Restless Nights

13 Tales of the Macabre

No Frills
<<<>>>
Buffalo
Buffalo NY

Printed in the United States of America

Albert, Michael S.

Restless Nights/ Albert- 1st Edition

ISBN: 978-0-9910455-6-3

1. Restless Nights – Macabre – Short Stories.   2. Suspense/Horror
No Frills – Fiction.
1.   Title

No Frills Buffalo Press
119 Dorchester Buffalo, New York 14213
for more information visit
nofrillsbuffalo.com

To my wife Melissa,
without whom all other things fade in meaning

I would like to express my warmest thanks to John Schreier,
for his intelligent insights and editorial input on this collection
of stories.

Contents

137. ***Gray Sky of Summer:*** Two teenage friends visit an abandoned house for fun but run into a mysterious old man who sends them digging in a local cemetery for a surprise that will change their lives forever.

151. ***Just Dessert:*** A man with only a few months to live takes revenge on his perennially obnoxious sister-in-law.

165. ***Unlucky Shot:*** Man's best friend helps solve a brutal murder in a most surprising way.

172. ***The Party:*** A terminally ill woman reflects on her life, suicide, and euthanasia during her last days.

183. ***The Wager:*** A bet made many years ago among friends about who would live the longest, leads to an unexpected ending for the last survivor.

189. ***The Undertaking:*** A group of young friends decides that breaking into a local funeral home one night would be an adventure; unfortunately for them they were right.

Restless Nights
13 Tales of the Macabre

A Collection of thirteen short stories from
Michael S. Albert

Edited by John Schreier

A KNOCK AT THE DOOR

"At least the table looks good."

It did – everything was shiny and perfect. The other preparations were coming along, too, though there was much still to do. With luck, they would have it all ready in time.

And then: "Grrrrrr -GRRRRR!" loud and louder!

"What on earth was upsetting the dog?"

"Here's a biscuit... what's the matter? You don't want it? If it was a steak you know she'd take it!"

The growling continued, at first a mixture of a whine and a low rumble then slowly building to a more menacing tone. The hair on the dog's back stood on end as she glared at, but did not approach, the door.

"Marie, I told you to put that decrepit dog to sleep months ago!" her husband Charlie said as he hand mashed the last batch of boiled potatoes, splattering small clumps of warm soft spuds on his red suspenders that seemed to just barely hold his ample belly in place. The aroma of roasting turkey and cooling pumpkin pies gently washed over the room gently stirring everyone's appetite. The bucolic scene unfolding in the kitchen stood in stark contrast to the sudden violent rainstorm that began to engulf the region. A Caribbean hurricane had made its way up the coast and was now taking out its fury on their part of the world. Local creeks were flooding and most of the smaller roads were covered in thick slick mud and partially obstructed by fallen trees and branches. Only a few circuitous roads, mostly known only to the local residents, remained passable. This effectively isolated the rural community of Janesville for the duration of the storm.

The lights dimmed for a moment then went out. A moment later they flickered back on as heavy rain and fierce winds rattled the windowsills. A mixture of hail and heavy rain bounced off the roof or was thrown into the side of the house by gusts topping fifty miles per hour. The howling wind screamed through the large willow trees in front of the 1870's farmhouse. Brilliant blue flashes of lighting lit up the room casting shadows of the sad looking trees on the house walls.

The farmhouse had been in the Calandra family for more than five generations. Its dining room was crowned by an oak beamed ceiling and enclosed by exposed fieldstone walls. Solid hardwood maple floors were present in every room. There was a traditional eighteenth century french wooden table that could seat twelve when needed. In the expansive family room a Bellagio fireplace was surrounded by architectural stone and capped by an ornate carved wooden mantel that rested on rolling pilings that accompanied a sturdy Venetian granite hearth. A beautiful oil painting encompassing three generations of Calandras hung above the fireplace and was the focal point of the room. The content and smiling faces painted by a gifted local artist seemed out of place on such a stark and ominous day.

"Not only is she half blind and arthritic, now she's senile and hallucinating," said Charlie as he added the home churned butter to his mashed potato mix.

"Charlie, it sounds like your description fits you more than Sophie," Marie said with a smile as she gently stroked the back of the large German shepherd, finally calming her down. Sophie was a 13-year-old retired police dog. The Calandras had taken her in more than a year ago when a close friend, a retired detective, died unexpectedly. She had some medical problems that came with her advanced years but she was a lovable and loyal dog.

The ceilings creaked as the Calandra's three grandchildren played hide-and-seek in the closets that connected the upstairs master bedroom and the adjacent guest room. The two boys, Jacob six and Robert eight, were rifling through dozens of shoes and dresses as they chased their younger sister, Madison, from one room to the next. Thunder occasionally boomed loud enough to shake the walls and cause the children to shriek and run downstairs for temporary comfort and assurance. They'd been told it was only the angels bowling but today the intense bursts of sound caused them to doubt that explanation. Once their fears were allied they headed back up the spiral staircase and disappeared in the back wing of the house for another game.

"What a terrible, terrible night," Jennie, the Calandra's oldest daughter, said as she entered the kitchen with hair still dripping from her recent shower. Marie reluctantly looked up from the simmering gravy she was meticulously stirring as if total concentration on the task would block out her anxiety about the storm.

"The temperature must have dropped twenty degrees this afternoon. I don't recall it being this cold and windy so early in the year in a long, long, time. Now Jennie, where is Jack? I thought your husband would have been here by now," she remarked.

Just as her last words echoed in the room, Sophie stood up and howled into the air before settling back down next to Charlie's tufted black leather wingback chair. The dog was continuing her unusual behavior. Perhaps the storm was upsetting her. She was usually happy to sleep away the evening, rousing only for dinner or for a short walk around the property. Certainly tonight there would be no walk. Only those with a strong motivation would dare venture outside in this inclement weather.

"The humane thing would be to put that poor dog down," Charlie mumbled to himself while sipping from a glass of Meridian Chardonnay. Holidays always made Charlie a bit grumpy. All the formality, cleaning, cooking and requisite small talk exhausted him, not to mention the cleanup. Truth be known, he would be happy to be in his robe and slippers having a microwaved frozen dinner, smoking a Macanudo cigar and reading the newspaper. All this fuss, over a turkey, he thought. He never understood it and was sure he never would. He secretly hoped for an early evening so he could read in bed before slipping into a peaceful slumber. He thought a few more glasses of wine might help that dream become a reality.

"Jack will be here soon mama, don't worry. He had a few errands to run in town. I think he was also going to help a co-worker replace a broken sump pump... not a good night for a sump pump to fail. I'm sure the weather snuck up on him and has probably slowed him down. I wouldn't be surprised if a tree or two hasn't fallen along some of the back roads. This isn't exactly the city and clearing the roads might take days. It will take time for him to find one in decent enough shape to make it back. With this weather cell phone service might be out and he can't call, who knows?"

"Well, on a night like this I'd like to see him here, with us, safe and sound. Especially with those horrible things going on around these parts…" her voice trailed off to a whisper as she recalled the recent newspaper articles and television reports. In fact, she had just heard an update on the matter this afternoon on the radio.

She was referring to a series of grisly murders that had occurred over the past six months. Four entire families, including children, killed in a most brutal manner. The police had no suspects, and the crimes appeared random and unprovoked. The only thing tying these horrible crimes together was the victims' profile. Families seemed to be the target. The city and surrounding towns were in a panic. The last murders, just a month ago, had occurred only twenty-five miles from the Calandra's remote farmhouse. There had been only one survivor, a nine-year-old girl. From her hospital bed she could only describe a tall muscular man with short beard and dressed in black clothes. She said he had angry eyes … eyes full of hate… the eyes of a wild animal.

"Isn't that just terrible? I heard he used an ax and… mercy, I just can't talk about this anymore. Even children slaughtered… body parts all over, it's too upsetting," Jennie said as she carefully placed the Waterford crystal glasses on the table. She then went into the kitchen to check on her cream of squash soup, it was almost done. Just the right consistency she thought. Jennie hoped her husband would get here soon. She didn't let on, but was starting to feel just a little anxious, especially with her mother reminding her about those murders… those were the type of things Jennie preferred not to think about. In her mind that kind of depravity only happened in places like Texas or Florida or the mountains of Montana. It happened to runaways or to girls who drank too much and went home with the wrong person, or to people hiking alone in remote places. It didn't or at least it shouldn't happen in quiet farming communities. Not to hard working God fearing people.

Just then Sophie's hair bristled and she stared at the front door. Her ears were back and tail straight out. Her intense "grrrrrr" grabbed everyone's attention. A moment later a sudden knock on the front door broke the eerie silence and the entire household's attention was riveted toward the foyer.

"Who's there?" Jennie called out. There was no answer, only a distant rumble of thunder. Sophie grew increasingly agitated as Jennie cautiously approached the door. "Who's there I said!" Then finally, over the screeching wind, she heard,

"It's me, honey. It's Jack. Please open up. I'm getting soaked out here!"

Jennie exhaled then slowly pulled open the heavy oak door. It groaned as it swiveled on the rusty metal hinges. There stood her husband, unrecognizable, in a thick green parka, looking like he had just climbed out of a swimming pool. He walked toward the fireplace as Sophie cautiously approached him growling, with her upper lip quivering. Her dark brown eyes fixed on him... her body leaning forward and tail perfectly straight.

"What's the matter? It's just me ole girl. We'll have to get you a pair of thick glasses like Charlie's," he said, smiling as he dried his beard and hung the soaked parka on a brass hook near the blazing fire.

"What took you so long to get here?" Jennie asked as Jack walked towards the family room.

"Actually, I've been outside for a bit. I noticed one of the gutters was plugged with leaves, and water was backing up on the far side of the house. I was trying to clean it out before the roof starts leaking."

The big shepherd slinked away from Jack and moved cautiously toward the fireplace. She began growling at the coat. She sniffed and barked as if it were a feral animal that meant her harm.

"What is with her tonight?" Jennie asked a little exasperated. "She's been acting very strange the last half hour. I've never seen her worked up like this."

Jack answered, "Maybe she doesn't like the coat... the fur collar and all. I admit it's awful looking, not my style at all. I borrowed it from Gavin when I saw the weather turning for the worse. I was helping him replace his sump pump after work."

"I knew I didn't recognize that old stained coat. I thought maybe you dug it out of one of bags in the attic meant for the Goodwill," Jennie said sounding relieved to have Jack back at the house.

"Well I can give it back to him. On my way here he called me on my cell to say I dropped my wallet in his basement. He's going to bring it to me. I told him given the weather he could just bring it to work tomorrow, but he insisted. Maybe he can stay for dinner. It looked like he was going to spend Thanksgiving alone. I don't know that much about him, he keeps to himself at work. He's been there six months and doesn't seem to have made any friends." Jack parted the thick pleated curtains and gazed into the fog and rain. "I think I see his pickup parked by the barn. He should be here any minute."

Marie's heart suddenly sank. A simple thought had been mulling around her brain that had only just made its way to her consciousness. Sophie wasn't just any old police dog, she had spent her career as a cadaver dog.

Marie said nothing as she quickly left the room and frantically grabbed the phone to dial 911... her heart almost stopped when she realized there was no dial tone. She hoped upon hope it was the storm that had caused the outage... then, a loud knock at the front door. It resonated through the house mixing with the sound of the children running down the stairs. Marie had heard a thousand knocks on that door over the years, but this one was different. It didn't sound like flesh on wood... more like metal.

DIGGING FOR
THE TRUTH

I was upset, but not really surprised by how muddy the back roads had become. The spring rains had come harder and earlier than most years. The slick roads drew me across a large number of evergreens that stretched toward the forest floor as they were pulled from the weight of the rainwater. They formed an eerie canopy that both provided both a sense of security as well as one of entrapment. My breath came shallow and quick as I maneuvered my Jeep Cherokee around several large puddles of muddy water. With the whipping rain, fallen tree limbs, and having to dodge large areas of standing water, my nerves were shot. The dark moonless night made my headlights almost worthless. Even the fancy and very expensive halogen high beams did nothing more than paralyze a few deer unfortunate enough to cross my path. Worst of all, the incessant banging coming from my trunk was enough to make anyone's anxiety reach the panic level. Turning up the radio wasn't much help. I could feel the thump, thump, thump of the body hitting the sides of the trunk with each sudden turn that I made. There were times I thought I heard sounds coming from beneath the shroud but I knew it was only my brain, fried with fear and drenched in adrenaline that conjured up the noise. He was dead and that was one of the few things I could be sure of.

I was now several miles into Luther Forest, a 10,000-acre public wildlife preserve that was a mini version of Ontario's Algonquin Provincial Park. I could see the abandoned hunting cabin just off to my left, whose broken front window and absent door revealed rotting wood furniture and a rusted refrigerator. One could only imagine what other discarded items lurked inside. Whatever they were I had no time to think or to worry about them now. I was less than a hundred yards from the spot I had scouted the night prior. The only good thing about the rain was that it would quickly cover any tracks that I made. Not that anyone would be snooping around out here or have any reason to. But anyhow, it felt good to know that my tracks would never be seen. I needed any shred of good news I could find, just a little something positive to think about. A few minutes later I pulled up to the makeshift grave I had dug just twenty-four hours prior. I turned off the engine, leaving on the lights. I stepped out of the Jeep, and quickly surveyed the area. The rustling of something in the distance startled me. Then I remembered that there was plenty of life in this forest, most of it just not human.

The relentless rain had caused sliding mud and detritus to partially fill in the hole, so I had to get my shovel out of the car and prepare to dig yet again. I could see nothing was going to be easy tonight. I should have known better, as things had gone far too smoothly in the beginning. Fortune has a way of eventually leveling the playing field. I walked over to the hole and slid down to the bottom. I looked like a mud wrestler at the end of a losing night, and felt much the same. Each thrust of my shovel brought up soft mud and tore through webs of fine tree roots that resembled the legs of an emaciated spider. I'd wager that it would be well past midnight before I'd be done here.

I thought about the surreal situation in which I now found myself. How is it that a thirty-seven-year-old, successful family practice physician finds himself in the middle of these dank woods, at almost midnight, preparing to dump a body into a makeshift grave? It's often said that doctors bury their mistakes, but I don't think this is really what is meant by that quip. In a way, you might say it applies to my current predicament, but it's not exactly what you might think. If you queried me a year ago, I would have never bet I'd be in this situation. I never really saw myself as a high roller, maybe more like a card crimper. But things have a way of changing and fortune can be a very fickle friend.

The first time I set foot in Stoney Creek, was to look into buying an existing medical practice. I was almost finished with my residency training in family medicine and was looking for my first private practice opportunity. I had student loans to pay and needed to start making a living wage. Stoney Creek was a rural, upstate, NY farming community of about twenty thousand people. I drove into town along Route 229 South. I had my big book, twelve steps and twelve tradition books in my glove compartment, companions from a previous life I wanted to leave behind. I saw the magnificent red barns with their attendant dairy cows filling the landscape. There were vast expanses of vibrant yellow sunflowers, and green cornfields. Large rolls of bailed hay covered some fields, left there to dry in the warm afternoon sun. Apricot colored horses lazily chewed grass and one looked up at my slowly moving car with only passing curiosity. A group of young boys carrying fishing poles walked along the shoulder of the road. I could hear their joyful laughter as they disappeared over an embankment. There was a warm breeze in the air and I could look over the road and see a small stream (I later learned its name was Hasting's Stream), slowly meandering its way toward Lake Erie. From the beginning, I liked the feel of the place. To make it here I thought I needed just a bit of beginner's luck.

I drove into the heart of town. It had the typical landmarks lining the main street, which surprisingly was not called Main Street, but rather Fields Avenue, after one of the town's first and most beloved mayors. There was Arthur's Hardware Store and the Three Penny Café. The every small town's *Joe's Barber Shop* and the tall, red-bricked town hall with requisite Greek revival columns and tall sliding sash windows. The police station had parking spots for three cruisers and was next door to Josette's Beauty Salon. Across the street stood the bank and a block east was the middle school. A half a mile away and on the corner of Fields Avenue and North Park Street was Kurak's Funeral Home, the final stop for many of the town's folks and a place I would soon get to know better than I ever wanted. Stoney Creek Memorial Hospital, sporting a full service emergency room and seventy-five inpatient beds was a mile outside the town proper and not far from the one hundred acre county park. It was classic Mayberry for a new age.

Dr. Jim Harcroft's residence was an 1850's white Victorian house with red shutters that he had converted into a medical office more than forty years ago. One half served as his house, the other his place of business. He had two examining rooms, a waiting room with four chairs and an old black and white television. A few non-descript prints hung on the wall and a classical music station could be heard playing in the background. He had one nurse, Betty, and an elderly somewhat cantankerous receptionist named Mary, who doubled as his office manager. Harcroft was now in his late seventies and finally ready to retire. His children and grandchildren were no longer in town. He and his wife had a daughter, Mary Beth, who resided in Albany and they were planning to move down there as soon as he sold his practice. His son lived in Portland, Maine. He was a pleasant man and spent several hours with me going over the local politics, town history, and amenities of the region. As he peered at me through his bifocals he meticulously reviewed the finances of his medical practice and answered all of my questions in a very friendly and quite congenial manner.

I had worked as an accountant before deciding on medical school, so was a bit older than many of my fellow residents. This, however, had given me a business sense that few of my peers possessed. I was eager to settle down and would lay even odds that I could build a very stable as well as lucrative practice here. I hoped someday to be profitable enough to attract a partner. That would make the night call a little bit easier. After some negotiating and contract revisions by our respective legal representatives, I signed on the dotted line and that July became the local town doctor for the people of Stoney Creek, New York.

The first six months went by quickly. I was working twelve-hour days, making early morning rounds at the hospital and trying to fit in some semblance of a social life. I had been divorced for five years, my marriage the victim of my commitment to medicine, a few bad debts I had accumulated and an unhealthy fondness for whiskey and water. Given my now very hectic schedule, I never seemed to have the time to meet anyone. A few of my patients tried to set me up with cousins, sisters, and an assortment of their lonely friends. Most of the people I met were very nice, but nobody special emerged from the late night dinners, local corn festivals, or full-length feature movies. Nonetheless, things were moving along quite as usual when a chance meeting with one of my date's father changed the course of events in a way I could never have foretold.

I arrived early for my dinner engagement with Rosalie Bartullo. While I waited for her to finish her makeup I had a chance to sit on the back deck with her father, Alphonse. After a brief introduction, we shared a beer and made small talk. He discussed, at length, the concrete business he ran. Eventually, he told me about the fellow his daughter had previously been married to and how he was glad they didn't have any children. "Now I wanna be a grandfather like anybody else," he said, "but this bum she was married to, he woulda only caused trouble. A real nobody," he said leaning back against the speckled green granite island on the deck's outside kitchen. I could tell he adored his daughter, something I made sure I would never forget.

"I felt it the first day she brought him home," he said as he finished his beer. "I can tell by looking in a man's eyes if he's worth anything." I tried to avert mine, lest Alphonse make any snap inferences. He was certainly a man on whose wrong side you did not want to be.

"Well, I'm sorry to hear that. Rosalie seems like a wonderful girl," I said in a weak voice, feeling inadequate and not able to come up with anything more brilliant to utter at that moment.

"You bet she is! Here comes the princess now."

"Now, Daddy, what stories are you telling David?"

"No stories, dear, we was just getting to know each other a little."

"Well Rosalie, we had better get going, or we'll be late," I said as I put on my navy blue sports coat and cinched up my red linen tie, held in place with an impeccable Half Windsor knot that I learned to tie at an elite Christian Brother's prep school in my early teens. Our dinner reservations were in twenty minutes and I hated to be late. I would bet I'd have to break a few speed limits to get us there on time.

"It was a pleasure meeting you, David. Why don't you stop by the Egyptian Room on Saturday, it's our local club. A good friend of mine owns the place. It will give you a chance to socialize and meet some people," Alphonse said between lusty bites of his sausage and fried pepper and onion sandwich. He had a small bit of grease dribbling down his swarthy round face. He could also use a shave but I sure wasn't going to say anything.

"I think I might just do that. I've been so busy I haven't had a chance to meet many people outside of work."

"Then I'll plan on seeing ya around eight o'clock. It's on the corna of Lakeview and Allengrove Drive." He then put his large left hand on my shoulder and gave it a squeeze while he firmly shook my hand with the other. I could smell the odd aroma of a mixture of fried onions and Old Spice after-shave as he got close to me. "I look forward to seeing ya then."

"I'll be there," I said as Rosalie and I dashed to my Jeep under the watchful eyes of her overprotective father.

My evening with Rosalie was pleasant. We planned to attend a play together that opened the following week. In the meantime, I hoped to make some new male friends at the Egyptian Room. After all, I was in the market for a golfing partner, and wanted to get the scoop on the best local courses. I'd wager that my game was as good as or even better than any of the locals. I also needed information about the best contractors. I was planning some office renovations in the near future.

I arrived at the Egyptian Room a few minutes past eight o'clock. After entering the outer foyer, I could see Alphonse in the main room smoking one of his expensive cigars. He waived me over. "Hello, David. Let me introduce ya. This is Robbie, Kevin, Johnnie, Mark, Phil, and Danny," he said as he directed his open hand toward each man respectively. "A coupla others are at the bar getting drinks," he said with a smile. "And this, everyone, is Dr. David Feltzer. He's taken over for Dr. Harcroft, who in my humble opinion was getting a little bit too old and senile to trust him to put a finger in my ass!" He laughed explosively, joined shortly by the others.

"I heard last time he gave you a rectal examination he had both hands on your shoulders," Danny chimed in, almost choking he was laughing so hard. Everyone had a drink, and most smoked imported cigars. I saw the discarded bands in the mahogany rimmed ashtrays, nothing cheap here. Cohiba Esplandidos and Arturo Fuente Opuses hung from their mouths. The entire room had a heavy blue haze that burned my eyes. I wished to myself that I had brought Visine, but couldn't imagine using it in the company of my new acquaintances. I certainly didn't want to seem weak or frail in front of this crowd.

"Play cards doc?" Johnnie Calabesi inquired.

"Sure do, what's the game?" I asked taking a seat at the ornate mahogany table.

"We got lots of games. Let's start with Five-Card Stud. Chips are five dollars each."

"Wow, you guys don't fool around," I said thinking the ante sounded somewhat steep. I hesitated for a brief second, my eyes fixed on the beautiful blue and yellow Persian rug underlying the gaming table.

"Don't worry, your credit is good here. I'll guarantee your chips," Alphonse said with a large, toothy grin. He swallowed the rest of his beer, and ordered the dealer to start the game in his distinctive raspy voice.

By 3 a.m. I was pretty much drunk, my eyes perpetually bloodshot from all of the smoke, and over eight thousand in debt to my new friends.

"Well, doc, don't worry about it. Your luck is bound to change. The ponies is runnin' tomorra' and we gotta 'notha poker game planned for Wednesday," Alphonse said looking as though he had too much energy for this time of night.

I staggered home and fell asleep on my couch watching Casablanca on the cable classics station. My old habits and addictions were recurring, my year of counseling becoming a distant memory. The gambling and drinking had contributed to my first divorce. That, coupled with the long hours of studying, my marriage hadn't stood a chance. There was also that nasty embezzlement charge that cost me quite of bit in legal fees to keep me out of jail and to get the records sealed. Gambling debts were the root of that problem, and that particular addiction now threatened to make a mess of my new life. Before I knew it, I was a regular at the Egyptian Room, the racetrack, and quite a few private, high stakes invitation only parties. Within six months I was in debt over one hundred-fifty thousand dollars. I was laying out almost ten thousand a month just to keep up with the hefty interest payments. Alphonse was hinting that I needed to increase those payments to start bringing down the principle. The anxiety was keeping me up long into the night. There were days I would fall asleep at my desk in the middle of dictations or even dose off while talking to a longwinded patient. I fantasized about just taking off one day, and never looking back. In my heart, however, I knew Alphonse or one of his 'business associates' would find me, and then there would be hell to pay. Concrete shoes was not the foot apparel I wanted to be sporting.

It was about six o'clock on a Friday evening, and very unexpectedly my options were about to expand. It was a cold night and outside my partially frosted window I could see a few inches of freshly fallen snow on the railings leading up the stairs to my office door. My last appointment of the day had cancelled and I sent Betty and Mary home early. I noticed a large shadow move up the stairs out of the corner of my eye. A moment later, the doorbell rang. I opened the door to find the police chief, Jake Kurak standing on my front porch.

"Hello, doc. Sorry to bother you so late on a Friday. I'm sure you'd like to get home, but I needed to speak to you in private." I welcomed him in and offered him a seat in my office. Jake was the half-brother of Bob Kurak, the local funeral director. He stood over six feet tall with thin black hair and a large potbelly that forced apart the buttons on his uniform. I had heard he'd been a police officer in the town over forty years, and the chief for the past twenty, or more. Word around town said he was a tough son of a bitch, and the only person he trusted or was close to, was his brother

Bob. Even they had been known to have a volatile relationship, leading to a pretty serious brawl or two over the years, mostly over family matters or issues of pride. Lately, things seemed to have settled down and the two of them appeared to get along fairly well. That, at least, was the local gossip.

"Doc, let me be brief. Word around town is that you're heavy in debt to Alphonse Cinaquinto and his crew. Pretty steep debt, I hear," he said as he leaned close enough for me to smell the Chinese food on his breath.

"Well, I've had my problems, with playing games of chance, so to speak. It's true I owe some significant money, but I'm working on it. I plan to have everything squared away by year's end." I knew I didn't sound very convincing, but the conversation was starting to make me feel a bit uncomfortable. I considered it my private problem. One I could deal with on my own.

"Well, doc, I might have a solution to your problems, but anything I say here can never, ever leave this room. If it does, Alphonse Cinaquinto will look like a Boy Scout compared to me," he said as he stood up and looked directly into my eyes. Even though I felt very intimidated, I asked him to continue, assuring him our conversation was completely confidential.

"Doc, I'll be honest with you. I've had my law enforcement contacts do a pretty thorough background check on you. I am very aware of your previous problems, even the details of your divorce. That's one of the reasons I thought I would come and talk with you." I was relieved to see him sit back down in his chair. His thighs squeezed by the tight armrests.

"Please, then, go ahead." My stomach turned, not quite sure what I was about to hear.

"I have a plan that could clear you from your debt. It involves my brother Bob, you, and myself. It will mean half a million tax-free dollars for you, but I have to tell you, it is completely and unquestionably illegal. Not to mention, it carries significant risk on all our parts." Given my precarious financial predicament and my weekly phone calls from Alphonse or one of his friends, I had no choice but to listen. I'll admit jail looked better than an unmarked grave. Although very apprehensive, I was also extremely intrigued. Little did I know then, that in less than six weeks, the man sitting in front of me would be stone cold dead.

The next month saw several meetings between the Kurak brothers and myself. The plan was quite ingenious and I would play an integral role. We would have to be meticulous and need some luck, but as time went on and as we worked through the details, I slowly gained confidence. We always met late at night at the funeral home. Even trained as a physician, walking past bodies in caskets, many dressed in their Sunday best, was a bit unnerving to say the least. This was especially true since Bob always kept the lights turned out so as not to attract attention. I was always picked up by Jake in a hearse so no one would take notice of my car parked at the funeral home at such odd hours. I remember our last meeting before we set our plan into motion. I walked into the funeral home stumbling over an empty box as my eyes slowly adjusted to the darkness.

"Hello, doc," Bob called from the back room.

"Good evening Bob. I trust all is well," I said taking a seat next to the refrigerated morgue drawers. "Wow, it's cold over here," I said.

Jake laughed. "That's 'cause you're sitting next to the deep freeze."

"What's that?" I asked, somewhat bewildered.

"That's the cooler that freezes bodies. We use it for chilling bodies that are decomposed or cannot be identified and need to be kept around for a long time. It keeps them as fresh as possible for as long as necessary. I've got one in there now, care to see?" Bob asked with half a smile.

"No thank you, I prefer that my patients be above room temperature."

We spent the next hour rehashing every detail of the plan. We acknowledged the riskiest points and developed several contingency plans. I was mentally exhausted by night's end. Each of us was well versed in the roles we would play. If everything went perfectly as planned, the odds would seem to be in our favor, if only slightly. But, by my calculation, not ending up in prison was still going to be a long shot. It was however, better than the alternative.

"Well, we are all set then," Jake said adopting a more serious tone.

"I'm ready," said Bob.

"I can't think of anything we haven't covered," I added. The mood in the room turned somber, and I left to go outside, leaving the brothers alone for a moment. Eventually Jake emerged from the building and I got my chauffeur-driven hearse ride home.

A week later, at six o'clock in the morning, my phone rang. It was Jane Carlson from police dispatch.

"Dr. Feltzer I've got terrible news. I just got a call from Bob Kurak. He said he went to pick up Jake for a golf date this morning and there was no answer at his door. He broke in through a window and found Jake dead in bed! He said he was already cold, so he didn't bother calling the rescue squad. He wants to know if you could get over there."

"My God, that's terrible news! Call him back and tell him I'll be there in fifteen minutes. And Jane, could you call Francine Garlac, the emergency department supervisor and have her meet me there as well?"

"Sure will. I'll call her as soon as we hang up." I thanked her, got dressed and raced to Jake's place.

I arrived at the house five minutes before Fran. As I saw her pull into the driveway, I waved from the doorway. I quickly went to Jake's bedroom and she entered the house a moment later.

"Looks like he died in his sleep. Most likely his heart. I was seeing him as a patient. He didn't want anyone to know, but he had atrial fibrillation and severe aortic stenosis. I discussed referring him to Dr. Strenger at University Hospital for a valve replacement, but he wouldn't hear of it." Fran lifted his eyelids and shined a penlight, then listened for a minute for breath sounds and agreed.

"I had no idea he was so sick. Did you already call the coroner?"

"No, but I'll do that now. I'll certify it as natural and save the pathologist from getting involved. Bob said that Jake never wanted to be autopsied. He saw enough throughout his police career and made Bob promise he would never do that to him." I led Fran quickly out of the room. She went over to console Bob. "I'll be right back, I left my bag in the room." I returned a moment later to rejoin the other two. I then offered my condolences to Bob and proceeded to call the coroner to discuss the case. He agreed that given Jake's underlying health problems an autopsy was unnecessary. Bob said that he would arrange for the body's removal directly to his funeral home. With that, I left for the hospital, where I had to make morning rounds on my patients.

Jake's memorial service was quite moving. Several prominent citizens praised his loyal service to the community. Bob delivered a stirring eulogy. His ashes were laid to rest in Forest Lawn Cemetery on a crisp sunny Saturday morning. The mayor appointed an interim chief of police and after a few weeks, things started to return to normal.

Ten days after the funeral Bob phoned me and asked that I stop by his place. As soon as I had finished with my last patient, I closed the office and drove to his house. I rapped on the heavy oak door with its antique brass gargoyle knocker. A moment later, Bob answered.

"Come in doc, can I get you a drink?"

"No thanks, I've got a sick patient to attend to as soon as I leave here." Bob proceeded to lead me downstairs into a subbasement that had a drop down ladder. It was very dark, with only Bob's flashlight to guide us. The room smelled damp and the flashlight illuminated cobwebs and layers of dust. I took a seat on a musty, pink couch. I could barely see anything in the room. Bob seemed to be acting overly cautious. I took a deep breath. The weight of all we had done was finally hitting me. I heard an unexpected movement from across the room.

"How are you doing doc?" I was startled by a familiar voice. Across the dim lit room I saw the shadowy figure of Jake Kurak sipping from a glass of what smelled like top-shelf whiskey.

"Fine and yourself, Jake?" I said in a manner almost too calm for the situation.

"Not bad for being dead over two weeks," he said as he laughed a loud chuckle, which was soon joined by his brother. "By the way, doc, what was that shit you shot me up with? Man, it really knocked me off my ass!"

"I gave you a few cc's of Propofol, a neuromuscular blocking agent, Michael Jackson's sleep aid if you recall. An intravenous dose just before Fran came in was enough to paralyze your respiratory muscles and dilate your pupils. I needed to reverse it with a little Ritalin, which is why I had to get her out of there pretty quick. I didn't want her to witness any resurrections."

"And the medical records," Bob asked, getting more serious.

"I fabricated EKG's, lab work, and physical exams. I even documented Jake's refusal for heart surgery. His record is perfectly documented. Anyone reviewing his chart will be amazed he lived as long as he did."

"That's good, because the insurance company will be sending out investigators. It's routine policy for payoffs over five hundred thousand, and this one is for one and a half million," Jake said smiling.

"Well you carried that policy for over twenty years, so no suspicion there. The medical record looks legit, the death was certified by the attending physician and witnessed by a qualified nurse, and the body has been cremated. Mrs. Lico would never guess her husband Frank ended up as ashes in Jake's urn and that they buried an empty casket. I think our ducks are all in a row." Bob seemed pleased as he summarized the facts.

"Then what's next," I asked, feeling a bit uncomfortable at how smooth things had gone up until this point.

"Jake slips out of town in the middle of the night and makes his way to Buenos Aries, courtesy of a recent identity theft. On paper he is a completely new man, including passport and driver's license. He then sets up a temporary residence. In the meantime we endure the insurance investigation and then I collect the money from good old American Mutual."

"How long does that usually take?" I asked, having never collected on a policy.

"I should have the money, tax free, in hand in less than four weeks, then I'll set up three offshore accounts in the Cayman Islands, each with five hundred thousand dollars. You doc, after paying off your debts, will still have a nice start to a retirement fund. I'll work another year to make it look good, then sell the funeral home and join my dear brother in beautiful Argentina where we'll live like kings."

The next few days saw insurance investigators Russell Marcus and Ed Cadrone spending quite a bit of time with Bob and myself. They reviewed medical records, spoke to friends and colleagues, and consulted with their home office. Aside from being

35

a bit upset about Jake's cremation, they seemed satisfied that everything was on the up and up. They concluded their investigation and told Bob he could expect a check for one million, seven hundred thousand dollars. The extra two hundred thousand was due to accrued interest on the cash value policy. Things were looking even better than expected.

A few nights later I was in a deep sleep, the first good night's sleep I'd had in what seemed like months, when the phone rang at two thirty in the morning.

"Hello," I mumbled barely conscious.

"Doc, you gotta get over here right now!" It was Bob Kurak and he sounded absolutely panicked.

"What's the problem?" the adrenaline rush now bringing me to a state of hyper alertness.

"Holy Christ, doc, I killed Jake, I can't believe it, he's dead!"

"What happened? Calm down Bob. Tell me what the hell happened!"

"We started getting his things packed and had a few beers. Then we started getting heavy into the booze, starting with shots of whiskey. Jake can get nasty when he's drunk. He started bringing up personal things from years ago, so we started arguing, pushing each other, and then we started throwing punches. I hit him with a chair and he fell backwards down the basement stairs. At first he was talking, incoherent, but talking. Then he stopped. What was I supposed to do? I couldn't exactly call an ambulance."

"I know Bob, I understand. Are you sure he's dead?"

"Yes, he eventually stopped breathing, and he's all black and blue around his eyes. He's got blood coming out of one of his ears."

"Sounds like he fractured his skull. What the hell do we do now?" my pulse now racing, and visions of a ten by six jail cell started flashing through my head.

"We have to get rid of the body. You have to take him far out in the woods and bury him. If anyone finds the body, it's all over!"

"Can't you just cremate him?"

"No, there have to be special arrangements to use the crematorium. I already burned Frank Lico's body in place of Jake last time. That's way too risky to try again, especially with the insurance guys just leaving town. We don't want any red flags that would bring a return visit. Best to bury him in a deep hole out in the woods. A place where nobody can ever find him."

"All right, let me drive around and find a spot. It's raining like hell out there and I want to find someplace before the back roads get impossible to use. I can't believe this!" I was starting to get frantic.

"It's an incredible mess but if we stay cool, things will be okay," Bob said in a half- hearted attempt to calm me.

"I'll find a spot and get a hole dug. You bag the body and clean up any blood. Be thorough. Tomorrow night I'll pick up the body and bury it," I said not believing those words were really coming from my mouth.

"Okay doc, I'll get things straightened out here."

"And the extra money?" I asked, greed now replacing my sense of fear.

"We split it even. I think we deserve it after all of this." That made eight hundred fifty thousand each. The thought went a long way to settling my nerves.

"Okay, I'll see you late tomorrow night." I washed up and threw on a pair of blue sweat pants and an old gray sweatshirt. I tossed a pair of old rubber boots, a cutting spade, and a shovel in the back of the Jeep. I was beyond scared at this point, but realized I had to think straight if I wasn't going to end up spending ten years in a federal prison.

I spent the next two hours driving up and down the backwoods deep in Luther Forest. Finally I came upon an old abandoned hunting lodge. I got out and walked around. I pulled out a pair of binoculars and spent a few minutes looking around, even though the sun was now starting to rise, I couldn't see much. I thought I had seen a car following mine about a mile back with its lights out, but with the rain, I couldn't be sure. I had taken some sudden, deliberate turns and backtracked a bit. I looked around again and didn't see anything. The last thing I needed was those insurance investigators nosing around. I pulled the spade and shovel out of my trunk. I spent the next two hours digging a hole. Luckily, the heavy rain had loosened up the dirt.

When I was finished digging, the hole was pretty close to the standard six by three feet of real estate we all get in the end. Technically, Jake had a very nice funeral while he was still alive. I guess that helps make up for him ending up in some unmarked, backwoods hole, buried like a broken down old farm dog.

When I returned home, I had a hard time sleeping from the adrenaline rush and all the exercise. My head ached and my upper arms were throbbing from all the digging. Eventually, I fell asleep for an hour and was awakened at six a.m. by the alarm clock. I looked like absolute hell and a cold shower didn't do much to wake me up. I had a couple cups of coffee and a swig of Jolt Cola. I would have to be awake for tonight's work.

I finished up at the office early and had a roast beef dinner at Aunt Millie's Restaurant. I went straight home from there with my nerves twitching and did a lot of paperwork that I had been neglecting. I even read a few articles from the latest edition of the *New England Journal of Medicine.* I felt unusually productive, especially given the state of anxiety I was in. Around midnight, I finally set out for Bob Kurak's place to commence the dreaded task.

I arrived to see Bob waiting on the front porch smoking what looked like his second pack of cigarettes. Butts littered every stair and his fingers looked as brown as mud.

"Hi, doc, I'm sorry for this. I really made a mess. I can't believe I killed him…" His voice trailed off and he was sobbing.

"Listen, I'm real sorry about Jake, but we both really need to stay cool about all of this. Help me put his body in my Jeep. I'll take care of burying him, and you try to get some rest. I've got a couple Ambien in the car. Take them, they'll help you sleep."

"Thanks, doc, I appreciate it." Looking warn, Bob walked back into the house.

I pulled the car behind the house and then proceeded down the rear basement stairs. Bob had already covered Jake's now stiff body in a double layer of heavy green plastic wrap, with both ends heavily taped with gray duct tape. We both struggled with the body to get it upstairs and into the storage area in the rear of the Jeep. Rigor mortis had made it necessary to have his legs extended over the back seat. I reminded Bob to get some sleep and that I'd call him first thing in the morning, to assure him the task had been completed. The weather had again turned windy with heavy rain as I set off for the woods.

I tried, as I drove, to pull in a classical Toronto radio station but it was nearly all static. I settled for a zealous, fundamentalist minister that convinced me that I pretty much had little chance of avoiding damnation. My concentration was suddenly broken by a siren, then red flashing lights in my rear view mirror. I immediately pulled over, and just as fast, my palms began sweating and my heart thudded wildly in my chest. A town police car pulled in behind my Jeep and an officer got out. He stopped a few feet from my window when he recognized me. Luckily he holstered his flashlight when he sensed there would be no trouble.

"Good evening Dr. Feltzer. What brings you out so late on such a nasty night?" It was Officer Chad Bradley, a five-year veteran on the Stoney Creek police force. His parents were two of my patients so I knew him more than casually.

"On my way to make a late house call. Hoping to prevent a visit to the emergency room for one of my patients," I said, hoping to sound convincing and praying that the stinging rain and blackness of the moonless evening was enough for him to make his stay at my car's half opened window as brief as possible.

"Glad to see you're doing your part to keep the cost of medical care down. I run into a lot of over-indulgers at this time of the night. Sorry to have inconvenienced you. Drive careful in this rain."

"No problem at all," I said relieved as he walked back to his car, talked briefly into his radio and then drove off. I was thinking to myself how priceless the extra hundred dollars I had spent on deep tinted windows had just proved to be.

I turned off the main road and followed the path I had mapped out the night before. Rain was hammering on my windshield as thunder and lightning made the dark skies seem even more ominous. I tried to get my mind off the grisly task at hand and settle my nerves. I thought about a nice island vacation with a hot oil body massage and midnight lobster buffets. Every time I started to relax, a slight turn of the Jeep or a bump in the road caused Jake's body to bang against the side of the truck.

At last, I could see the abandoned hunting lodge I had established as my point of reference, I then drove fifty yards beyond it and brought the Jeep to a slow stop. I left on the high beams for some illumination, but they didn't seem to offer much assistance. I got out of the Jeep and walked around to the back, with the thick, rain soaked mud clinging to my boots. Each step was an effort. I opened the hatch and tugged on my morbid cargo until Jake's body fell out and onto the ground. It took nearly ten minutes to drag the body to what would now be its final place of rest. The heavy rains caused mud to partially fill in the lonely grave, which resulted in another thirty minutes of labor in re-digging the hole. I certainly didn't want a wandering hunting dog to drag parts of Jake home. I couldn't and wouldn't want to have to explain that in some dingy interrogation room.

The gruesome task was almost complete. I shoved the makeshift green body bag over the edge of the hole and heard a muted thud as it hit the bottom of the muddy tomb. I slid down next to the body to reposition it. The thunder and pouring rain made my headache worse, as I feverishly worked to finish this grisly task.

I'm not exactly sure when I noticed, or rather, sensed it. I suddenly felt as if something, or someone, was watching me. My heart raced as I turned and looked up. There, standing on the edge of the hole where I had just slid Jake's body in, was Bob.

"Hello, doc, nice job you did here with this impromptu grave. If circumstances were different, I'd consider hiring you as one of my gravediggers," he said sarcastically.

"What the hell are you doing here," I demanded. I then watched him raise from his side a .45 ACP Kimber handgun and point it directly at me. "My God, Bob, what are you doing? Insurance fraud is one thing, but murder!"

"It's a little late for the lecture on morality, doc, don't you think?" he nodded his head at the body bag. I was seized by the horror of the moment. I dropped to my knees and tore at the green plastic that covered Jake's head. There, confirming my worst fears, was a bullet hole in his forehead, clearly fired from close range. I turned back to Bob, silhouetted from the headlights of my Jeep. "Sorry doc, but once I cashed that insurance check and looked at all that money packed neatly in suitcases, I started to think that a million seven would look much more appealing than a paltry five hundred grand and change." With his free hand, Bob pulled on the slide of his pistol and chambered a round, then resumed his aim. I dropped my head trembling, and waited in anguished anticipation for a bullet to end this nightmare. I heard a sharp crack of gunfire echo from the rain drenched trees and seconds later felt Bob's warm limp body topple onto my own. Pushing him off, I noticed a large hole decorating the middle of his back with burnt edges on his now bloodstained blue dress shirt.

It seemed like an eternity passed, but in retrospect, I'm sure it was only a moment. I saw only smoke at first, then recognized the unmistakable scent of a burning cigar. Behind its glowing tip, stood Alphonse Cinaquinto looking down at me with a wide grin.

"Looked like you needed a bit of help, hope you don't mind me butting in." I was nearly in tears but did manage to ask how in the world he knew I was out here, in the middle of these godforsaken woods. "I make sure my boys keep a close eye on people who owe me the kind of money you do. They caught wind of what was going on a few weeks back and started keeping very close tabs on you," he said as he extended my own spade into the hole to assist me out. "Take a load off doc, Danny and Phil are in the car. They'll fill things in here, so to speak," he said with a hearty laugh. "I guess your debt to me is history, and you'll have plenty left for yourself, minus a small fee to cover the rescuing your ass expenses!" He put his arm around my shoulder and together we walked to my car passing Danny and Phil without saying a word. As we walked, I could hear the shovels of Alphonse's boys filling the grave. The distinctive smell of Old Spice was in the air.

Rosalie and I had a real first class wedding. Over 350 people from town were in attendance, including all of the local dignitaries. The reception lasted well into the morning, and concluded only because the band was out of songs, and we were out of energy. I never saw Alphonse happier. He smiled all night sucking on his Don Antonio cigars and drinking from a hundred-dollar bottle of France's best merlot. At one point, Phil and Danny led a spirited rendition of the Tarantella.

Life in Stoney Creek is very good. I'm still the community's favorite and only general practitioner. Rosalie eventually replaced Mary as my office manager, who had her retirement party just three days before we discovered that Rosalie was pregnant with our first child. I now frequent the Egyptian Room, almost as much as Alphonse. I even gamble a bit still, but he monitors my participation, making sure I don't play tables charging more than a dollar a chip. He smiles and says that he, "Just doesn't want to see me get myself into a hole that I can't get out of. After all, what are father-in-laws for?"

COLD REALITY

Damn it, I'm cold. I've never been this cold. What's happened to me? My mouth and tongue won't move. My thoughts seem frozen. I can see a slit of light, fuzzy like splayed out cotton, through my left eye, but just barely. I must have been in an accident. I vaguely remember the cold, a struggle... then complete darkness. I don't know when, yesterday, last week, I have no idea. I assume I'm in a hospital. The dirty white walls and what appears to be an examining lamp attached to a long white arm that juts out from its oversized base are a dead give- away. Only hospitals and police departments, whose clientele often have little choice in where they do business, could get away with such drab and unimaginative decor. Maybe I'm paralyzed... lying in a spinal cord injury ward. They should at least have the decency to send a nurse... to bring me some blankets or turn up the friggin' heat. Don't they realize that I'm cold? I'm damn near freezing. Somebody better get in here. Somebody better get here soon!

Suddenly, the gurney upon which James Nash laid motionless began to move. The sudden jerk caused his shoulder to bounce into the guardrail. He could see one large black hand grasping the left guardrail. The wheels squeaked like an old rusted grocery cart as he moved down the otherwise silent corridor and then through a steel gray door that opened automatically with a shrill hiss. A shudder ran down Nash's spine. *Oh my God, maybe I'm not paralyzed... maybe I'm dead! It would explain why I'm being completely ignored. The good news is that I'm not in Hell, not with this temperature, unless of course the good book has it all wrong... very wrong.*

46

Slowly patches of memory begin to return. I remember fishing, more specifically, ice fishing on Lake Michigan. After enduring a week of sub-zero temperatures it had finally warmed to a balmy forty-one degrees and the sun burned brightly. I was fishing with two of my best friends, Rick Tomzack and Earl Feifer. We were enjoying a few beers... OK, a few too many beers, and pulling in some reasonably sized perch on five-pound test line using salted minnows we caught the prior spring. We were laughing and telling embellished versions of last year's hunting stories when I heard the crack. The recent warming trend must have been enough to thin the ice. Rick stood up, took a step or two and then the ice tore away from our fishing hole and he disappeared under the water. Earl and I immediately laid flat down but the ice around us ripped violently apart. I remember the icy cold water... the shock of submersion and the intense cold and complete darkness. I attempted to orient myself and swim upward. I ran head first into the ice that blanketed the lake. I pounded my fists until they bled, trying to punch through the ice. My hands became numb from the cold. My lungs burned inside my chest and my heart pounded. My state of panic rapidly drained the small amount of oxygen from my blood. Involuntarily, my mouth opened, futilely attempting to suck air into my desperate lungs and finding only cold green water. My eyes searched for light that would signal an opening. I could find none. The cold penetrated my body. My limbs became rigid and the darkness slowly enveloped me like a shroud.

The gurney continued its monotonous journey, passing a plaque that dedicated Mason Memorial Hospital to the small community of fifteen thousand people that helped build the first rural hospital back in 1956. The powerfully built orderly opened a large oak door with a shade covered window and carefully wheeled in the stretcher. In a low baritone voice he said, "Hello, Dr. Rowley. This is Mr. James Nash."

"Thank you Herman." Rowley replied as he spun around in his wooden chair, the Listerine not fully covering the smell of whiskey on his breath. "Listen Herman, on your way out, please send in Gordon. I'll need a hand."

"Will do, Doc." After placing Nash on the examining table, Herman strolled out of the door, briefly stopping in Gordon's office to relay the message from Dr. Rowley. In a moment Gordon was in the room. He immediately put on a pair of blue surgical scrubs, grabbed several packs of sterile gloves, booties and hats and walked over to the doctor. Rowley had been in a foul mood all morning, but that was typical when he started his drinking before breakfast or never stopped from the night before.

Finally, a doctor is going to see me. Nobody has spoken to me. Maybe it appears I am unconscious. Maybe I am in a coma. I can't move a muscle, and I can barely see anything out of the small opening in my left eye. Maybe I need an operation. As best I can tell, I appear to be in an operating room: large tubes, metal trays and an array of silver instruments. Too bad I didn't get a chance to pick my surgeon. I'm sure my HMO is happy about that.

Rowley finished dressing in his surgical scrubs and staggered over to the table upon which Nash lay motionless. "Gordon, do you have the patient's chart?" Gordon looked up from the form he was completing.

"No Dr. Rowley. I'm sorry, I don't. It is somewhere between the ER and medical records." Rowley was visibly upset.

"How the hell can I do my job? This is ridiculous!" he shouted.

"If you like sir, I can go and attempt to track it down."

"No... that could take an hour. Do you know anything about the patient?" Gordon approached the table across from Rowley.

"Some kind of water accident. A group of ice fisherman fell into the lake. Otherwise no significant medical history. I believe he's forty-one. Two others were brought to St. Elizabeth's down near Strykersville." Rowley took a deep breath and let out a sigh that signified his disdain for the incompetence that always seemed to surround him.

"Well then let's get started. With any luck the chart will eventually find its way down here before we're finished."

I felt hands begin to examine me. They felt my head and my neck, pushed on my abdomen, then examined my neck, chest and limbs for broken bones. X-rays were then taken. They pulled up my eyelids to examine my eyes. It was then that I saw it. A nametag swung before me. My body tingled with fear and terror rushed through me in a way I had never known. I read it again in disbelief. The ID badge read: James Rowley, MD, Coroner's Physician. That moment I understood. They are preparing to autopsy me. They think I'm dead! I have to find a way to signal them... to let them know.

Gordon attached the new blades to the wooden scalpel handles and handed one to Dr. Rowley. "All right Gordon, let's begin." They cut through the skin near each shoulder and extended the incision deep into the subcutaneous adipose tissue and muscle. They completed the Y-shaped incision and began to peel back the flap of chest skin to expose the rib cage. Taking a large pair of bone cutting scissors, Gordon separated each rib from the attached cartilage until only a few shreds of muscle and fibrous tissue connected the chest plate to the rest of the body.

Oh my God... what are they doing to me? They're cutting me up like a piece of beef. The pain is excruciating, beyond description. I'm trapped. This can't be happening. Maybe I am in Hell!

First, the sharp incisions from the scalpels, followed by the breaking and cutting of each rib. Not even someone's worst nightmare could have prepared James Nash for the medieval-like pain he was now feeling. It was as close as this century had to offer for a live disembowelment.

The chest cavity was now exposed. Rowley removed one of the lungs but was unprepared for what he next saw. Out of the corner of his eye he spied a slight quiver from inside the sac that surrounded the heart. Startled, Rowley stood back, one of the lungs slid from his hand and landed on the floor with a soft thud making its own thick red puddle. Could it be? A faint irregular heart beat? He thought about stopping...but what would the others say? Reports of his drinking had caused him enough trouble with the medical staff. He didn't need this to come out. After all, he was the pathologist. Shouldn't he be sure someone was dead before he autopsied them? He could already hear the pointed questions at his disciplinary hearing. But he had examined the body… there was no sign of respiration or heartbeat. Even drunk he couldn't make this big a blunder. No corneal reflex… the body temperature was eighty-nine degrees for God's sake. In thirty years of practice he had never seen anything like this…perhaps it was some sort of agonal reflex, not yet reported in the literature… but it looked like a heartbeat. Unlikely as that sounded he knew what he had seen. "Gordon, step away and bring me the Stryker saw."

"Dr. Rowley, we're not ready to remove the brain, why do—"

"Just do it, Gordon! Goddamn it who's the boss around here?" Gordon shook his head and abruptly left the room to obtain the saw. Rowley then quickly reached around the heart and severed the aorta and pulmonary artery and then quickly cut the vena cava and pulmonary veins, thereby completely detaching the heart. The heart pulsed one last time in his hand before he slid it still quivering into a waiting bucket of formalin. He felt sick but continued the post mortem… having just ensured the *mortem* part of that term.

Precocious third year medical student Frank Abrams read the chart with astonishment. As part of his emergency room rotation, he was to review the charts of any patients arriving DOA, then attend the autopsy and give a synopsis of the pathologist's findings the next morning during clinical teaching rounds. Mr. James Nash's chart was fascinating. It had taken several hours to track down the chart as it passed through various bureaucratic channels, eventually finding its way into Medical Records. He flipped through the pages… forty-one year old male, submerged in thirty-seven degree water for twenty-nine minutes. Pronounced

51

dead on arrival due to drowning. Abrams had read about rare cases of what was termed "profound hypothermia". It was reported mostly to occur in young children: body temperatures under ninety degrees, mimicking all the signs of clinical death, imperceptible pulse and respiration, heart beating less than ten times a minute. If the doctor caring for the patient had never seen a case, a live patient could easily be mistaken for dead. Someone suffering from profound hypothermia needed to be monitored with equipment sensitive enough to detect their faint vital signs and be gradually warmed to normal body temperature over a course of many hours. If done correctly, most of the patients recovered, often completely and without any neurologic deficits.

Abrams was suddenly overcome with a sense of profound dread. He raced down four flights of stairs and the three corridors leading to the autopsy suite. Gordon stood over the body, his surgical scrubs covered in blood and small bits of tissue. He was sewing the body together to prepare it for the funeral home. Dr. Rowley emerged from the dressing room in his outdated gray suit. "Well, Mr. Abrams. It's so nice of you to join us, however you are a bit late. Typical for a medical student."

"I'm sorry, I was helping sew-up several lacerations in the ER and it took quite a while to track down the patient's chart."

"Lucky for you, nothing too interesting… a run of the mill drowning. I'm sure you'll see one or two more before you graduate, especially with spring only a few months away," Rowley said as he tried to hide the slight tremor in his hands.

"I thought it might be something unusual, a case of profound hypothermia." Rowley laughed then looked across his desk at his exhausted looking assistant.

"Gordon, these medical students are always the same. They hear the sound of hoof beats and think zebras, when horses are much more likely." Abrams looked askance at the old pathologist and turned to walk away. Rowley called after him, "Mr. Abrams, if you really want to be industrious you could take the forty-five minute drive over to St. Elizabeth's. The two other drowning victims were brought there. Give Dr. Thompson, the St. Elizabeth's pathologist, a call. I'm sure he'd be glad to review the organs with you. Too bad you couldn't assist, but I just phoned them and told them to get started as soon as possible so we could have a joint conference with the news reporters early this afternoon."

Although Rowley didn't mention it, he had also strongly recommended the other less experienced St. Elizabeth's pathologist start the autopsy with the head rather than the chest as was customary. Rowley had lied and said he had found subtle cerebral trauma that might be missed if the brain wasn't examined first. In truth, Rowley certainly didn't want them to have the same surprise as he had. The disturbing memory of the beating heart squirming in his hand like a frog snatched from a pond was still fresh. If by chance one or both of the other drowning victims were discovered to be profound hypothermia cases, it could raise serious questions about his case not to mention his competence. A good medical examiner from the city, trying to make a name for himself, would surely want to launch a thorough investigation. The forensic team might start looking real close at the autopsy findings. It would be better just to tie up any loose ends and report these cases as unfortunate recreational drownings. He sure as hell didn't need anyone screwing up his last year of practice with endless inquiries, depositions and medical negligence hearings. He had worked hard all his life and deserved to collect on his well-earned and very lucrative pension. He wasn't going to let a little mistake at the tail end of his career put his comfortable retirement at risk.

Abrams tuned pale and sprinted to the nearest office with a telephone. He frantically dialed the number for St. Elizabeth's, his hands sweating as he punched each number. He felt light headed and his hands tingled from the anxiety. After several rings an operator answered, "St. Elizabeth's, could you hold please?"

"No! I absolutely cannot." It was too late; there was only 1980's pop music on the other end of the line.

In the morgue at St. Elizabeth's Hospital, the bodies of Rick Tomzack and Earl Feifer gazed vacantly at each other with half opened eyes, like fish on ice at the local seafood market; the terror in their hearts finding no way of expression. Dr. Thompson stepped up to one autopsy table while his senior pathology resident stood adjacent to the other. Suddenly the silence in the morgue was broken. The phone began ringing in Thompson's office. "Shall I get that Dr. Thompson?" the resident asked looking up from the body.

"No, that's OK. We should be finished soon. You know what they say: if it's that important, they'll call back. Besides, always remember there are no emergencies down here. That's one of the perks of our profession." Each chuckled then made their first incisions along the skin of the scalps, the first steps in removing the brains.

THE CORPSE
THAT TALKED

All things that live their lives,
by taking flesh for food,
Shall one day find that they
in turn will feed the maggot's
brood.

James Davis was lost, but to his mind that was too harsh a conclusion. He just didn't know exactly where he was. His new white Lexus glided along each curve of the asphalt road with little effort. It was now more than half an hour since he passed the black Ford pickup truck. That was the last vehicle he saw as he sped into the horizon.

It was nearing midnight and the sky had grown black and looked increasingly ominous. Clouds covered then uncovered the moon like some celestial game of peek-a-boo. The car continued past the vague outline of rolling hills covered with small bushes and interspersed ash, cottonwood and occasionally maple trees. He hadn't seen a gas station or roadside diner in over thirty miles. The gas gauge read just below quarter of a tank. He was getting very hungry. He needed to find someone who knew where the hell he was. A wrong turn somewhere led to this mess. He really regretted not bringing his GPS. The directions seemed so simple at the time… just around the next bend he spied his first sign of life so to speak, a cemetery, and he chuckled to himself. The gravestones were overgrown with grass and weeds. Several were cracked or overturned. He approached the dirt road leading up to the black wrought iron entrance gate, which stated he was entering "Oak

View Cemetery." He could see that most of the headstones were worn and faded. The names were mostly eroded away or illegible. Only a date here and there could be made out on an occasional marker. There was nothing past 1948 that he could see. It didn't matter that much, it wasn't the graves that interested him. It was what appeared to be a small brick caretaker's house in the near distance. A small light shone from one of the closed windows. He hoped someone was home. He was hungry and really needed to get something to eat. Some directions would also be helpful. He got out of the car and walked into the cool night, leaving the engine idling and the lights on to provide some degree of illumination. He slowly walked the forty yards of unlit roadway to the oak door that was surrounded by two white pillars. He gently tapped the door with the heavy brass knocker. There was no response. He knocked harder and the sound reverberated through the house. Still there was no answer. He slowly turned the oversized knob and partly opened the heavy wooden door.

"Hello? Is anybody home," he asked somewhat tentatively. Again, he was met with only silence. The light he had seen emanated from a back room. The front of the house was completely dark. He turned on the flashlight he had astutely retrieved from the glove compartment, walked further into the house and looked around. The kitchen cabinets were dust covered as were the whitewashed oak baseboards. A few dishes were in the cast iron sink and several cockroaches scattered when he shined the light on them. The doorway leading to the backroom was partially blocked by cobwebs. He could see the cemetery from the back window. The clouds had passed and now the moon was full and bright lending an eerie glow to the larger monuments. He slowly entered the back room. It was lit by a bare bulb, suspended from the ceiling. There was a simple birch wood desk and chair in the far corner. A few time-worn and yellowed papers were strewn about the desktop. An ancient looking black telephone sat on the floor. The phone line was long ago chewed away by hungry rodents. Mice droppings decorated the table tops and the pungent smell of urine seeped from the cheap linoleum floor, or at least what was left of it.

Suddenly the room's silence was shattered as the front door opened, spinning on its hinges and bouncing forcefully off the adjacent wall. A moment later James Davis found himself staring into a darkened room and just being able to make out the outline of a tall heavy-set man that was pointing a 12 gauge Winchester Defender in his direction. "Please don't shoot," Davis said in a voice much calmer than the situation would warrant.

"Who the hell are you and what are you doing here?" the heavyset man shouted in a slightly nervous voice.

"My name is Jim Davis. I'm lost and I was looking for directions to the nearest town. I'm low on gas and getting a little desperate. I saw a light and was hoping to find someone here."

"Little chance of that. I'm Artie Shaefer by the way, RT for short," he said as he slowly lowered the gun to his side. "I have a house just over the hill and happened to see someone poking around in the old cemetery house. Every once in a while we have a problem with vandals, so I took it upon myself to investigate. The place hasn't been used in years, but I put in a new light bulb now and again, so to make it look like someone's here. Helps keep away the undesirables. A group of misfit teenagers tried to dig up one of the graves a few years back... some kind of depraved senior year prank."

"Sorry to have caused you any trouble. Like I said, I'm lost, hungry and getting pretty low on fuel. I wasn't sure when I would run into another gas station so I took a chance and stopped here."

"Maybe I can be of some help. Old man Stillman has a farmhouse about twenty miles from here... just continue on route 33 west. It'll be on the right. Now, I haven't talked to him in quite a while mind you, but as I recall he has a small barn that he converted into a guesthouse, for the in-laws I think. He might be able to put you up for the night. Things will look better in the morning and I'm sure he'll be able to get you some gas and direct you back to the main highway. I'd put you up in my place but the wife don't take well to strangers."

"I really appreciate the information," he said. The big man scratched his belly as he pulled up his overalls and said in a quiet voice,

"Oh, and one more thing, don't let him scare you. He has a reputation of being... well, a little odd I guess is the kindest way of putting it."

After the snack Artie provided, Davis climbed into the Lexus and slowly drove out of the cemetery. He was feeling better. The thought of getting some decent directions helped his mood tremendously. He turned onto route 33 and was back driving along the lonely stretch of road on which he had already spent too much time. A half an hour passed and he saw the old farmhouse about a quarter mile away. A small propane porch light lit the house's facade. It was a large gray cedar, two-story colonial style residence. Davis wondered if the owner would be awake. It was after eleven o'clock and none of the interior house lights were on. The guesthouse was similarly vacant looking. He left the car and quickly ascended the four stairs to the porch. He knocked once and the door squeaked opened, the handle apparently broken long ago.

"Hello, Mr. Stillman?" Davis said in a questioning voice as he poked his head inside the doorway.

"You don't have to shout!" Davis swung around and saw someone sitting alone in a side room, slowly rocking in an off white wicker chair. It was a tall gaunt man with sparse gray hair. He stared at the visitor in the doorway.

"My God, you scared the hell out of me," Davis said, but still appearing very calm.

"You're the one sneaking into my house at this ungodly hour. If anyone ought to be scared it should be me!"

"Forgive me, I tried to knock and the door opened... I didn't mean to..."

"Well what's your business here," the old man said sharply as he stood up slowly, never taking his eyes off his unexpected guest.

"I've gotten myself very lost and I need a place to put up for the night."

"It's been a long time since I took in a boarder... not since Margaret..." his voice trailed off and his gaze became vacant. "I'll tell you what mister..."

"Davis, Jim Davis."

"Mr. Davis, why don't you have a seat over there. It's an old chair but sturdy, like myself. I don't get much company, and don't sleep very much at night. A few hours here and there if I'm lucky. I guess a doctor would call it insomnia. I just don't like the dreams I sometimes have. I see Margaret, my dead wife and... it's just too depressing."

"I'm sorry to hear that." Davis answered sounding more tired than sympathetic. Every word he uttered was deliberate and slightly slurred.

"You know what I miss Mr. Davis?"

"What's that?" he answered trying to sound interested.

"I miss being scared... really scared. Ever since I was a kid I loved roaming around dark musty basements, hiding in cornfields at night, and reaching under the bed without looking first. As kids we'd climb the fence of the local cemetery and play hide-n-seek among the stones. The fear... the adrenaline made me feel alive. Margaret was the same way, God rest her soul. We'd have a hell of a time thinking up ways to scare the bejesus out of each other." Davis looked on, somewhat surprised at what he was hearing. "So I have a proposal for you. You can spend the night and to boot have an old style country breakfast in the morning if..." Stillman then paused for a moment to light his pipe and continued, "if you tell me a very scary story."

"A scary story? I don't think I know—"

Stillman then interrupted. "Oh come on Mr. Davis. Everybody knows a scary story." Davis squirmed a bit looking uncomfortable with the request.

"It's an unusual thing you ask," Davis said feeling unsure of what to do.

"Well your car is in the driveway and I'm sure there is a gas station in the next thirty or forty miles… course it probably won't be open at this time of night," he said with a wry smile as he puffed his hand-carved pipe, sending cherry scented smoke into the air.

"Mr. Stillman I really don't fancy myself much of a storyteller."

"Please, call me Ben, no need to be so formal."

"OK Ben, I'll give it my best shot, but I hope you won't hold me to a very high standard." He finally sat down in the only other chair in the room, and when he did the cushion let out a small puff of dust. Jim thought for a few minutes about the only scary story he could remember from his high school days when he'd sit around a campfire and drink beer someone stole out of their parents' fridge. "There were these two teenagers parked in a desolate area of Lover's Lane. The rock and roll music on the radio was interrupted by a bulletin. A madman with a hook for an arm had escaped from a nearby asylum—"

Stillman, slightly agitated interrupted, "No, No, everyone knows that story! Tell me something original. Something different."

Davis let out a heavy sigh. He looked straight into the old man's eyes.

"All right, Ben. Then how about this one? It was five o'clock on a Friday afternoon. Dr. Max Earlman, the hospital's chief pathologist, was hastily signing the day's biopsy reports. He had one eye on the paperwork and the other on the clock. He was leaving the next morning for a ten-day vacation to Germany. He and his wife had planned this trip for the past six months. He still had last minute packing to finish and was already an hour late getting home. As he packed up his briefcase the phone rang. He debated not answering it, but his sense of duty won out.

"Hello. Hello? Max, I'm glad I got you." It was Mason Hendricks, the hospital Vice President for Medical Affairs. "Listen, I need a favor. A really big one. There was an MVA and the driver was killed. A forty-something year old accountant. The coroner is in California for the weekend, his father is having emergency surgery. Could you do the post mortem tomorrow?" Earlman rubbed his forehead, visibly upset.

"Mason this is the worst possible timing. I'm leaving for Europe tomorrow at 7 a.m. Dr. Jackson is covering for me but doesn't have any forensics experience."

"I'm in a real bind, Max. Is there anything you can do?" Earlman slumped in his chair and thought for a moment. This was one shit storm he'd rather not be caught in. His options were limited and Hendricks had done him some important favors in the past.

"Well, maybe I can get it done tonight. I guess Jean could finish packing for me. I'll put in a long day and have at least the preliminary findings done by the end of the night," he sighed, a depressed look coming over his weary face.

"I'd really appreciate it," Mason said knowing how much the situation was upsetting Earlman.

"Remember this when my contract comes up for renewal," the pathologist said trying to lighten the mood.

"I will, and thanks again, Max." Earlman made a quick call to his wife explaining the unfortunate turn of events. She grumbled a bit but understood the predicament her husband was in. He told her not to wait up for him and he immediately tried to track down Hal Gorman. He was a medical technologist that also served as a diener... an autopsy aide, when needed. He called the Clinical chemistry lab hoping to find him.

"Mary, is Hal around?"

"Sorry Dr. Earlman, he left half an hour ago. It's his tenth anniversary and he has a six o'clock reservation at Lombardo's restaurant."

"Shit! I can't catch a break tonight. Well, I'll just have to do the post by myself. It will take a little longer, but I don't have a lot of choices at this point."

"Sorry, Doc," she replied, genuinely sounding sympathetic.

Earlman reviewed the E.R.chart and police report. Decedent was forty-five year old man who was an accountant with a big ten corporation. No significant health problems. Took a curve too fast and rolled over his forty-thousand-dollar luxury vehicle. The police report said the car was not in too bad of shape, unlike the occupant. If he was wearing a seat belt he might have walked away. No pulse on arrival in the emergency room. Attempts at resuscitation lasted one hour, obviously without success. If Earlman walked across the street to the police impound he could see the car itself. He didn't think this would be necessary. It was now approaching seven o'clock. He would be lucky to start the autopsy in the next forty-five minutes. If all went well he might be home just before midnight. He hoped that tomorrow he'd be able to sleep on the plane. Anyway, he wasn't going to let this last minute glitch spoil his vacation. The hospital began to look desolate. Much of the staff had gone home leaving the much smaller evening crew. He took the elevator to the sub-basement, and began walking down the long concrete floor that led to room SB-221, the morgue. The hallway was lined by discarded hospital equipment, antiquated hospital beds, and C.P.R. training mannequins (some looking a bit too life-like at this time of the night). He stopped in front of the oak door with frosted glass that read, Room SB-221, NECROPSY, etched in partially faded black lettering. Earlman pulled out a large silver key and slipped it into the lock. He was tired and considered putting the autopsy off until the morning. Hal would be available to help… he could catch another plane on Sunday. No, he decided, might as well get it done. *Just do it…* like the commercial says.

He opened the door and fumbled along the wall for the light switch, which he found after mistakenly hitting the fan and air conditioning switches first. The room had a musty smell of stale air. The unmistakable acrid odor of formalin was also present. Across the room the hum of the body refrigerator could be heard. It kept the six drawers a comfortable 40° F for the occupants. Earlman pulled open the first drawer revealing a small package wrapped in a plastic shroud. A stillborn baby. Drawer number two was empty. He pulled open the third drawer and there lay the body of an adult male. He matched the name and date of birth on the toe tag to the emergency room chart. This was his case. The decedent's clothes were in a bag on top of the body. He rolled a gurney from across the room and oriented it parallel to the morgue drawer. He slid two belts under the body and pulled first the head and trunk and then the lower extremities onto his cart. He took a moment to catch his breath. This was hard work and was usually done by the diener, a fancy name for an autopsy assistant.

He rolled the body over to the steel autopsy table and repeated the cumbersome transfer of the corpse. Once the body was securely on the table, he turned on the suction apparatus and hoses that would wash away blood and tissue fragments. He turned on the overhead light. He walked to the small bathroom and prepared to take a shower. It was a ritual he had performed with each autopsy over the past 30 years. A shower before and after. He understood the after one, especially with some of the putrefied bodies that forensic work sometimes brought. He was sure there was a good psychological reason for showering before, maybe when he retired next year he would pursue psychotherapy. He'd been suffering from generalized anxiety and occasional panic attacks for the past four or five years. Maybe a good psychologist could help straighten him out.

He walked into the small adjacent dressing room and disrobed. He stepped into the shower and turned on the water. It was cold as always. He began soaping himself up when he heard it… a groan… perhaps just the water flowing through the old pipes. He continued to shower… then again… that noise. A low-pitched groan. Yes, definitely a groan. He quickly rinsed off, dried himself and put on his blue scrubs. He walked into the morgue and listened. Nothing. After a moment he relaxed and approached the corpse on the table. He grabbed a pair of scissors and began to cut away the white plastic shroud. He gazed down at a man who looked only to be asleep. Only some large bruises on the chest hinted at the major chest trauma that lay beneath. He turned on the overhead microphone and began to dictate.

"The body is that of a forty-five year old white male measuring seventy-three inches in length and weighing one hundred ninety pounds. The head is atraumatic, the hair full and…" suddenly the lights flickered and after a few seconds, went out. "Damn," Earlman mumbled to himself. He waited a moment for the backup generator to go on. Then he remembered the morgue was not hooked up to the emergency power. That was reserved for the patient care areas. He remembered seeing a Macrolight flashlight on one of the tabletops. He walked over, turned it on, and miraculously it worked. There was enough light to get by, although he had never conducted an autopsy using a flashlight in the thirty-five years he had practiced pathology. He suspended the flashlight over the table and tried to concentrate on getting finished. He bent down to the corpse's face and lifted each eyelid. The unusual lighting gave an eerie sense that the eyes were staring at him. For a second, he thought he saw the pupil change diameter, but that was impossible. He proceeded to pierce each eye with an 18-gauge needle and withdraw a few cc's of clear vitreous fluid for toxicology studies. As he withdrew the needle from the left eye, he felt the cadaver's right hand move from the table and brush up against his leg… it startled him, and he jumped back. His imagination was starting to embellish reality, at least that's what he told himself. The arm probably just slid off the table, it was wet. The lighting was also poor… he probably accidentally bumped into the arm while withdrawing the vitreous fluid. He decided to take a break and compose himself. He was tired and very stressed.

He walked over to the small bathroom and washed his face with cold water. He took a deep breath and was getting ready to resume the autopsy when he heard the unsettling clang of falling metal. The instrument tray had fallen over... scalpels, scissors, forceps, all strewn about the floor. His nerves were now completely rattled... sweat beaded on his forehead and his pulse began to race. For a moment he wanted to lock the bathroom door and scream, hoping to alert security. Then he calmed himself, told himself the things a rational mind likes to believe. It was late, he was tired, he had a big trip in the morning... everything together had pushed his anxiety level into the stratosphere. He rubbed his face and slowly opened the bathroom door. He looked across the room to the body on the table after seeing the instrument tray on the floor. It was not immediately apparent how this happened. The window located against the adjacent wall was open, the wind swirled outside and the rain was getting heavy. Perhaps a gust of wind... that might... no, would explain it. He hurried to reassemble the tray. He lifted the scalpel and made the deep Y-shaped incision into the chest and deftly cut along the subcutaneous tissues. After using the rib cutters he removed the chest plate and found a thorax full of blood. A ruptured thoracic aorta due to blunt force trauma. There was nothing unexpected. Probably wasn't wearing a seat belt. A quick examination of the abdominal and pelvic cavities revealed nothing significant. Toxicology results would take a few weeks. He felt removing the brain was unnecessary, as the cause of death was quite obvious. He took representative tissue samples from the major organs for later microscopic examination. He then began to sew the chest together with coarse black thread and a long curved needle.

No need to be perfect, the funeral directors will remove it during the embalming process anyway. Earlman was feeling better. The weather was getting worse, but he was essentially done with the autopsy. It was just after 11 p.m. He washed the blood and tissue fragments off and placed the instruments in a bucket containing dilute Clorox. He then covered the body with a new plastic shroud. The funeral directors would be in at 7a.m. to retrieve the body so he felt no pressing need to return it to the morgue refrigerator. He'd leave the air conditioner on high. They might be a bit pissed, but hell they could call him in Munich to bitch him out.

Earlman removed his scrub suit and shoes and took a long shower. The cool water rejuvenated him and he imagined himself under a remote waterfall on a faraway island... surrounded by lush green vegetation, with exotic birds soaring between trees... his blissful daydream was suddenly interrupted. It was that groaning sound again... then the sound of something... moving about... perhaps the wind again ... or maybe a security guard on rounds... it was low pitched and monotonous... footsteps? Earlman didn't move. He turned off the shower... standing naked as he listened for it again. His heart raced and hands began to tingle... someone... something was approaching the bathroom. He moved closer to the door, leaning his ear just inches from the knob. Footsteps. Should he call out? He was frozen with fear... they were coming closer... getting louder. Then they seemed to diminish... moving away toward the morgue's entry door. Then they stopped. Next a sniffing sound... then that groan again... and the footsteps grew louder... coming back. Shuffling slowly... getting louder. In a moment they stopped outside the bathroom door. Earlman grabbed the handle of the door and held it tightly closed. He was hyperventilating, his hands slipping from the sweat. His eyes wide open and legs trembling.

"Who is it?" he cried out. There was no answer. Desperate with fear, the room beginning to spin... he pulled back on the door, flinging it open. He looked for a moment in disbelief. Then his heart began to pound, his chest became heavy... his breath gone. Everything went black as he collapsed to the floor."

"Hmmm... I liked it, Mr. Davis. Not the scariest story I've ever heard mind you, but it's good enough for a bed tonight and some breakfast in the morning." Stillman slowly rose from his chair and looked at Davis. "Mr. Davis, I'd like to show you something, would you wait here?"

"Sure, although I wasn't completely through with the story, there's still the epilogue."

"OK. Go right ahead."

"Well, it turns out that the security guards come busting into the morgue around 1 in the morning. Seems they got a call from Doc Earlman's wife when it started getting real late and Earlman still hadn't shown up. They find him stone cold dead, sprawled out on the bathroom floor. As they get closer they noticed a funny thing, there are large pieces of his flesh missing, torn off right down to the bone... and the autopsied corpse was missing. Just some blood drops and smudged red footprints leading out the door. One of the Jamaican security guards looked pale. He said his great grandmother used to say the souls in purgatory that were turned away from heaven would animate the newly dead before going to hell... and these walking dead would not be the drooling, brain-dead zombies of George Romero fame. They had the same cravings for human flesh, but would only animate recently deceased bodies. They outwardly appeared normal, which made them all the more dangerous. They were almost human. Now that's the end of the story," Davis said as he stood up from the dilapidated chair.

"Not too bad for a story off the top of your head... maybe you should be one of those horror fiction writers," Stillman said in his most sincere voice.

"You wanted a scary story, but you didn't say anything about it being fiction." Stillman turned towards Davis just as the visitor's sport coat opened, revealing the large coarse threads that held his chest plate in place. Davis was on top of him in a second. Stillman screamed, he tried to lessen the indescribable pain he felt by thinking of the wife he would soon see again... he looked away as Davis tore the skin and muscle from his bones, lapping at the pools of blood like a ravenous dog. When finished, Davis shuffled back outside towards his Lexus, which still looked good, dents and all.

At the same time, thirty or so miles away, at the Oak Lawn Cemetery's caretaker's house, Dorothy Shaefer discovered the partially mutilated body of her husband Artie, or RT if you prefer. Her terrified screams fell on the decaying ears of the cemetery's inhabitants. Luckily for her there were no *fresh* graves. Unluckily for her, as she bent over on this desolate night to frantically attempt mouth to mouth resuscitation on her fallen spouse, she didn't noticed her husband's left hand beginning to twitch.

UNSEEN
ADVANTAGE

Dr. Howard Ducray opened his worn Cabrelli briefcase. The cracked brown leather case had been his companion for more than thirty years, a gift from his parents when he completed medical school. Even in his sixties, he still fondly remembered his forensic psychiatry training at the University of North Carolina. He pulled out several thick bundles of paper and again reviewed the police reports on Otis Schenk. He slid on his gold wire-rimmed glasses that had been perched on the top of his balding head. What remained of his thin graying hair was matted in various irregular configurations. He slowly rubbed his short-cropped beard, growing coarser with each passing year. A trip to the barber was in order but lately he just didn't seem to have the time. He carefully sipped black coffee from a blue, southwestern style ceramic mug. The cup sported a picture of his English Mastiff, Sigmund. Including his tenure as chairman of psychiatry, he had spent more than twenty years working at the Fairmont Psychiatric Center located along the banks of Lake Erie, in upstate New York. There he had treated schizophrenics, bipolar disorders, manic-depressives and a host of other psychiatric ailments. Over the last ten years he had spent a great deal of time expanding his knowledge in forensic psychiatry. However, nothing learned or experienced could have prepared him for his next patient.

In the adjacent holding room, two uniformed police officers closely guarded Mr. Otis Schenk. He was the chief suspect in what the national press had dubbed the "Vampire Slayings." Eleven murders occurring over two years. The details were horrific, affecting even the region's most seasoned medical examiner, Dr. Weston McKay. Ducray swallowed his last mouthful of coffee, slipped on his favorite gray sports jacket, then took a deep breath and walked down a sterile appearing hallway to the holding room.

The two officers politely nodded upon seeing Ducray turn the corner and walking towards them. He gave a perfunctory smile back.

"Would you like one of us in there with you?" asked the larger of the two men, his thumbs hooked in his thick black leather belt while his large feet maintained a wide stance to support his massive frame. He leaned gently against the cinder block wall as he watched Dr. Ducray approach the room.

"No, thank you. I'd prefer to keep my first meeting with him as non -threatening as possible," said Ducray as he adjusted his glasses and loosened the knot on his yellow silk tie. Unconsciously he gripped his briefcase tightly as the guard sorted through several keys then unlocked the door.

"All right, but be careful, Doc. This guy's a real strange one, real strange. We'll keep an eye on things from out here. If there is a problem, we'll be right in." Ducray nodded and slowly opened the heavy metal door. He stepped into the room and behind him the door shut automatically with a heavy snapping sound, causing him a brief startle. He took a quick scan of the very ordinary room. It had a dirty white tiled floor decorated with a variety of unidentifiable brown and yellow stains. It appeared this room was off limits to the janitorial staff. The walls were covered with sheets of thick yellow foam held in place by layer upon layer of gray Duct tape. A single rectangular overhead fluorescent shop-light provided the only source of illumination. Otis Schenk sat in a brown birch wood chair, his hands and ankles shackled. He wore the standard issue blaze orange jumpsuit with the word Prisoner in bold yellow letters embroidered on the back. His eyes were closed tightly and his face contorted into what could only be described as a haughty smirk. Ducray seated himself in a similar chair five feet away, directly facing his new patient, with only a simple wooden table separating them.

"Good morning, Mr. Schenk. I am Dr. Ducray. I am a forensic psychiatrist. I was asked to talk with you this morning. Is that okay with you?" Schenk slowly opened his eyes and stared blankly at Ducray. His bloodshot eyes now held wide open, while he sat stiffly in his chair. The light flickered and Schenk smiled demonically, then pulled his chapped lips apart revealing razor sharp teeth that he had filed to fine yellow points. He remained quiet. Ducray quietly asked again if he would like to talk.

"What about Doc? Is this the shrink visit I get before they fry me and not feel bad about doing it? Or, do you want to talk about why I like killing people and washing in their blood?" Schenk followed his questions with a forced laugh, deep and menacing. "I'm a parasite, Doc. Simple. Most living things on this earth have one. I'm just a parasite to the human race, trying to do my part to cull the herd. There are too many damn people on this planet. God sent me to do this job. I help out when His disease, wars and natural disasters fall a little short. It's never enough, but I try and do my part. Too many people. It's starting to affect the ozone layer and shit like that. Air pollution, water pollution, and now even noise pollution. Your grandchildren will thank me one day. Got any grandkids doc? I like children, a lot, the younger the better." Schenk then dropped his head and started to sob, murmuring incoherently about children. He then moved his head around in large circles and began laughing.

"Maybe I didn't do any of this shit they're accusing me of… maybe I'm just some patsy. Like Lee Harvey Oswald."

Ducray leafed through Schenk's chart for a moment then asked, "Why don't you tell me about Dunkirk and the house you grew up in, Mr. Schenk?"

"You want to know about that whore mother I had? She hated me. The other three she had when she was young, with the same man. But my father was one of her "Johns". She never knew which one. You know doc, what I remember most when I was young? It was that she would buy all the other kids ice cream cones, but not me. I had to watch them eat it. Not once, but every goddamn time. She'd take us to the park and I'd be left in the car to watch the other kids play on the swings and slides. She said I was bad, and didn't deserve to have any fun." As he leaned back on his chair the sleeves of his jumpsuit slid up revealing numerous thick purple scars. According to his medical chart, some were self-inflicted, others not.

"I'm very sorry to hear that. It must have been a great source of sorrow for you."

"Yeah, but I got used to it. I made sure I never cried in front of her. I wouldn't give that bitch the satisfaction. I just made believe I didn't exist. It's screwed up, I know. I felt best when I would lie in bed, imagining I was dead. The pulled up bedcovers were the lid to my coffin. Down deep though, I knew I was smarter than all of them. My only joy in life was doing bad things and making it look as though one of my sisters had done it. I once

flooded the toilet by stuffing tampons down. I lived for that shit.
Then I'd laugh in my room while they got the belt. The louder they
screamed the bigger my hard-on got. I think the Devil's got the best
job in the world, spending his time thinking up ways to torture
people for eternity. Now that's entertainment!"

Ducray listened carefully, then redirected the conversation.
"Tell me a little about your stepfather." Schenk stuck his tongue
out, it had been tattooed black, and then he made a screeching
sound, then fixed his unblinking eyes directly on Ducray.

"He wasn't all that bad, drank too much, but pretty much
left me alone. I think he may have been screwing one of my sisters,
but I could never be sure. I was sixteen when he died. Strange
thing about that, when my mother had him placed in the coffin, she
had him put in naked. Not a stitch of clothes. I laughed about it at
the time but, now it seems... unnatural." Ducray spent another half-
hour exploring Schenk's formative years. His childhood was
abysmal and his teenage years not much better. Although he
couldn't rationalize the violence, he was beginning to see what
caused the putrefaction of Schenk's soul. They spoke another half
an hour then Ducray gathered his notes.

"Okay, why don't we take a break for now, and we'll talk
again tomorrow?" At first Schenk didn't say a word, just sat across
from Ducray with a wide toothy grin pasted on his face. When
Ducray reached the door, Schenk turned his head towards him.

"Hey doc, did you ever taste blood? I mean someone
else's? It's salty and metallic at first, but once you acquire a taste
for it, it's better than a three-dollar bottle of beer. The younger the
sweeter, no time to get all polluted."

Ducray didn't answer and left the room without looking back. He could hear Schenk laughing uncontrollably in the background as he walked down the hallway and eventually outside to his car.

Ducray grabbed a pastry from the waiting room outside his office. He slumped in his overstuffed executive chair and removed his phone from his jacket pocket. He scrolled through his sleek black iPhone and quickly punched in the numbers. In a moment he heard the phone ring in his headset.

"McKay here," the voice said on the other end, sharp and to the point.

"Hi Weston, it's Howard. Can I stop by this afternoon to go over the Schenk case with you? I just finished my first interview with him and need to fill in some blanks."

"Sure, I'll have Mary pull the autopsy reports and DNA results. At least what's available."

"Thanks Weston, is three o'clock okay?"

"That's fine. I'll see you then."

Ducray hung up the phone and went back to Schenk's chart. He was first diagnosed with schizotypical personality disorder as an older adolescent. Depending on how well he stuck to his medication regimen he might have one or two relapses annually, and then end up in either jail or an acute care psychiatric facility as a result. He was very intelligent and had an IQ of 160 on the Stanford-Binet. Under other, less macabre circumstances, he would easily have been a candidate for Mensa. Now aged thirty-one, Schenk was charged with a vicious string of homicides. He had a reasonable shot at using an insanity defense, but the prosecution could convincingly argue the type of murders and evasive tactics used to avoid being apprehended, demonstrated rational thinking and behavior. Ducray grew weary thinking about Otis Schenk, and needed a diversion. He put the case file aside, and spent the next hour reviewing a paper he was submitting to the *Journal of Pharmacopsychiatry.*

When his mind and nerves had settled, he got up from his desk, and strolled over to outpatient psychiatry. The clinic had bright yellow walls and an ivory speckled Berber rug. There were several paintings of sailboats and waterfront scenes that lent a peaceful aura to the room. Patients would come here to have their blood drawn in order to monitor the serum levels of their medications. They would also have minor medical problems attended to by the physician's assistant, Franklin Beauregard.

"Hi Franklin."

"Afternoon, Dr. Ducray. How are you doing?" Franklin asked, looking tan and fit, he looked the picture of a California surfer. His stethoscope was draped stylishly around his neck, and he held several patient charts under his arm.

"Doing well, thank you, how are all of our patients?" asked Ducray as he helped himself to a sip of bottled San Pellegrino water.

"Not too bad. A few are here for their routine lithium level checks and one has a strep throat. Phlebotomy has been crazy! I must have drawn blood on nine people this morning, and Mrs. Haley there, is here seeking a referral for cataract surgery," he said nodding towards an elderly, well-dressed woman in a wheelchair.

"Why don't you have her see Dr. Steinman? He does a good job with our patients."

"Will do, thanks. I heard the news about Otis Schenk. Believe it or not I actually met that guy a few times. I drew his blood when I moonlighted for the visiting nurses association. I also met him at one of the downtown clinics I used to work at. When he took his meds and attended therapy sessions he did pretty well. When he didn't he could be one weird dude, but I would have never figured him for the things he's accused of."

"Yes, I can't say much about it. The DA's office is trying to keep a lid on things. They don't want the press to turn this into a circus. He's being held in the forensic unit for the time being. In fact, I'm on my way over to the ME's office to discuss some of the details of his case."

"When he was off he was one of the toughest clinic patients I had ever seen, when he would show up for his appointments, that is," Beauregard said mentally recalling one of the times security was involved in dealing with Schenk's outbursts. "I guess I'm not totally shocked, but I always figured he'd end up a suicide, or overdose on drugs, or one of those people who takes out his entire family."

"Well, patients often have a way of surprising us."

"That, they do," Franklin said as he prepared to enter a treatment room.

Ducray said goodbye and walked outside. He secretly hoped he could remember where he parked his car. Feeling foolish, he wandered the parking lot, on what was turning out to be a beautiful spring day. Eventually he found his silver BMW and drove the ten miles through the inner city to the corner of Goodard and Genesee Streets, the office of the Medical Examiner. He arrived fifteen minutes early for his appointment with Weston McKay, the county's chief M.E.

The Medical Examiner's office is an expansive brown-brick building that stood three stories tall. Forensic pathology, including the five autopsy rooms and associated laboratories were located in the basement. The DNA, trace evidence, and serology laboratories were on the first floor. The next two floors housed ballistics and an assortment of administrative offices and conference rooms. Weston McKay had a large office at the south end of the third floor. The back wall of his office consisted of a large picture window overlooking adjacent Colonial Park. A handful of the countless awards McKay had received over the years haphazardly lined his rich cherry bookshelves. Also on display were pictures of Dr. McKay pressing flesh with local politicians and other noted dignitaries. A beautiful 75-gallon saltwater fish tank was built into the wall opposite his desk, which housed an array of brilliantly colored fish and a unique assortment of other aquatic life. The aquarium lent a serene atmosphere to an otherwise bleak, heart-wrenching profession.

Howard Ducray pulled his car into the back parking lot. Taking a moment to organize his briefcase he thought back to his meeting with Otis Schenk. He entered through a basement door that only frequent visitors knew existed. He showed his identification badge to one of the security guards who gave a familiar smile and nod then he entered the main corridor which housed the autopsy suites. He passed a bloated body with several freshly sutured incisions of the chest and abdomen with plastic tubes protruding from every orifice, the telltale signs of a fatal motor vehicle accident with an unsuccessful attempt at resuscitation. On a gray steel table, three small packages wrapped in plain white blankets, signaled that Dr. Ducray was in the presence of infant fatalities from SIDS, and other far less natural causes of death. He poked his head into one of the autopsy rooms. Trying to speak above the noise of a Stryker saw he shouted,

"Is Dr. McKay around? Hello, is McKay here?"

A staff pathologist looked up from the table. He was opening a victim's skull to enable a detailed examination of a bullet tract that traversed the frontal lobes of the brain.

"No, he left for his office about ten minutes ago," came his muffled reply. The pathologist was clad in several layers of protective garments that made him difficult to understand. Ducray thanked him, shut the door, and took the south elevator to the third floor, and walked down to McKay's office. Weston was staring out of his office window finishing a freshly buttered blueberry bagel, which he considered one of life's culinary pleasures.

"Hello, Weston."

McKay turned and smiled. "Afternoon, Howard. Grab a seat. Hope you had lunch. I don't think you'll have much of an appetite after reviewing the details of this case." Weston walked over to his drawers of hanging files, opened one, and pulled out a thick folder. He sat in his leather chair and opened the folder spreading crime scene photos over his desk. Ducray stared at them without blinking.

"Holy Christ, this guy was more sadistic than I thought," Ducray said, wishing now he had skipped lunch altogether. The pictures spread out before him depicted a gruesome story. Each one painted a desperate picture of a life lost in an unimaginable way. Men and women slaughtered like wild beasts, their bodies bound, beaten, and mutilated. The first four murders showed signs of only blunt force trauma. With victim number five, the bloodletting began. All of the subsequent victims showed evidence of repeated strangulation and sharp force injuries. Most victims were devoid of blood, and exhibited apparent teeth marks on the neck and scalp. When police sources leaked some of the gruesome details, the press dubbed the killer the "Lakeside Vampire" and began referring to the crimes as the "Vampire Slayings."

After a moment, Weston said, "The first break in the case came when laboratory technicians discovered blood from two individuals at crime-scene number five. The trend continued through number eleven."

"And they're a match for Otis Schenk?" Ducray said with some hesitation.

"Let me get Ed, our lead molecular man to explain." McKay called into the intercom base on his desk that attached to his telephone. "Ed, could you stop by my office? I'd like to discuss a case with you."

"Sure, be there in just a sec," A high-spirited voice promptly answered. A few minutes later a thin, balding man wearing a stained white lab coat entered McKay's office. He looked much younger than his forty years.

"Dr. Howard James Ducray, meet Dr. Edward Charles Drone," Weston said with a sense of false pomposity. "Ed took over a few months ago when director Joseph Coupton retired. Ed is Harvard trained and did a post doctorate stint at the Salk Institute.

Dr. Ducray is the chief forensic psychiatrist from the Fairmont Psych. Center. Sorry to say, his medical degree is from Yale!" Weston, a Harvard Medical School graduate, said smiling.

"Pleased to meetcha, whose head are ya here to shrink?" Drone said with a chuckle.

"Actually no one, but I have office hours on Wednesday should you need one," Ducray shot back.

"Thanks, Doc, but I find that a swig of whiskey and Gilligan Island reruns pretty much take care of any problems I have, but I'll certainly keep you in mind if the liquor store ever goes out of business."

"You do that," Ducray said with a soft laugh.

McKay stood up and interrupted their conversation, "Let's get back to this case. Dr. Ducray is interested in the Lakeside Vampire case."

Ed stood up and addressed the group, "Well, we found in addition to the victim's, one individual's blood consistently present at the majority of the crime scenes. This began with the fifth victim. Presumably this blood belongs to the killer. That conclusion is based on the science of variable number tandem repeats, which uses a class of satellite DNA from highly polymorphic regions of the genome. We used standard Southern Blot Analysis to compare the samples. The results showed blood present at the majority of the homicides belonged to a single individual, and that DNA is an exact match for one Mr. Otis Schenk." Ed pulled out the photographs of the gels and pointed out the details to the psychiatrist.

"Well, that seems like pretty damning evidence, but I'm just a bit surprised," observed Ducray.

"What do you mean?" asked McKay sounding a bit incredulous.

"Well, his behavioral profile just didn't fit. The crimes were all well thought out and appear very organized. Murders committed by paranoid schizophrenics are usually spontaneous, and disorganized. There is rarely an attempt to cover them up. Often the perpetrator doesn't realize they've done anything wrong or may not even remember the crime."

"I hate to impugn your psychoanalysis, but there's even more," Weston said as he dug deeper into the folder. "This information hasn't been released to the press. It's still considered privileged."

"What have you got?" Ducray asked now looking a bit defeated.

"Semen found at two of the crime scenes matched Schenk's DNA as well," Drone answered. Ducray looked at the others and admitted that behavior profiles and psychiatric methods were not hard analytical science, and certainly not as accurate and specific as DNA fingerprinting.

"There was one strange thing," Drone interjected, "finding the perpetrator's blood at so many of the crime scenes is very unusual. Furthermore, it wasn't found in the typical splatter pattern, as you would expect to find when blood is drawn during a fight or a violent struggle. The blood was literally mixed in with that of the victims'."

"How do you explain that?" Ducray asked, now even more confused. McKay walked back across the room and began pacing. He picked up one of the crime scene photos from his desk. It grotesquely illustrated a large pool of blood next to a victim with skin that appeared almost as white as cotton.

McKay answered, "We theorize that he would cut himself, then wash with the blood of his dead or dying victim. Mixing the blood in some sort of depraved ritual. He also apparently had intercourse with two of the victims after he had slain them. As I mentioned, the semen DNA matched that of Schenk."

After the meeting, Ducray decided to go home rather than returning to his office. As he drove, he recalled the scars he had seen earlier that morning on Schenk's forearms. Considering that and all that he had just heard from McKay and Drone, he thought that unless Schenk was fortunate enough to get the O. J. Simpson jurors, he was sure to fry.

Drone returned to his office, which was situated off a small corridor adjacent to the main laboratory. He sat in his office looking somewhat perturbed. He attempted a game of chess with a computer-based opponent with the moniker, "The Grandmaster." After a few minutes he lost interest. He didn't let on that he was bothered by what Ducray had said about the behavioral profile of the killer and how it didn't fit Schenk. Maybe Schenk wasn't what he seemed to be. In his upstairs office, Weston McKay was troubled by similar thoughts. He preferred all the evidence lined up, with one piece bolstering the next. Behavior profiling was certainly not hard science, and came nowhere near the analytical record that DNA fingerprinting had accrued over the past ten years. His colleagues often joked that DNA fingerprinting was the greatest advance in forensic medicine since the blowfly maggot. Still the discrepancy bothered him. He also wondered if there was something about Schenk they were missing. Had they taken the easy road and just followed the evidence without thinking hard enough about it?

After spending an hour by himself, Drone suddenly burst out of his office, "Boys, can you pull me the PCR reports, southern blots, and blood swatches from the Lakeside case?"

"You got it boss. You want everything?" asked Douglas Evans, a longtime technician of the crime lab.

"The last seven or eight should do it," answered Drone.

"I see the steam coming out of your ears and that wild look in your eye, what's cooking?"

"Just a long shot, a very, very long shot," he smiled and scampered back to his office now ready to finish his game of chess.

Upstairs, McKay spent the next two hours reviewing every detail of the autopsy reports. He went so far as to pull out the microscopic slides and reviewed each one. When he finished with that he reviewed all of the crime scene photos. When he next looked at the clock, he couldn't believe it was almost nine o'clock. He straightened up his office and locked his file cabinet drawers. As he left he saw another figure crossing the parking lot. Ed was just leaving the building as well. He ran to catch up with him.

"Hey Ed, is this overtime approved?" he said jokingly.

"You know I'm salaried, so don't sweat it!" answered Drone, playing along.

"How about a beer at One Eyed Jack's?" offered McKay.

"Only if you're buying."

"I'm buying. What else is new?"

One Eyed Jack's was a blue-collar pub on the north side of the city. It was average size with ten large wooden tables, most sporting hand carved initials from patrons long gone, and a variety of witticisms collected over the years. The pub offered up a variety of homemade micro-brewed beers with names like Tar Stew, Reindeer Red, and Czech Pilsner. They also served a staple of traditional and exotic imports. Each was served by big Mike Marshall, a three-hundred-pound Vietnam veteran with an array of tattoos and a long gray ponytail. Marshall might have looked rough, but he held a master's degree in classical studies from Boston University. Above the bar hung an aged sign that read "*Abandon hope all ye who enter here*", a reference to Mike's favorite book, Dante's *Inferno*.

"Well gentlemen, what's the county's brain trust doing here? I haven't seen you fellows in a few weeks. Things must be getting lively at work, eh?" big Mike snickered.

"Now I know why you work here and not the comedy club," retorted Ed.

"How about a couple of Old Peculiars to start? We'll be at the far table," said McKay.

"I see your taste is improving as the years pass, yah must be getting good advice from your patients. I'll have 'em sent over in a jiffy. A coupla Peculiars for a coupla peculiars," Mike said laughing at his own play on words.

"Thanks, maybe we'll even leave a tip this time," Drone said with a friendly smirk.

"Don't start any new traditions on my account!" big Mike answered with a hearty laugh making his triple chin quiver in delight.

McKay and Drone spent the better part of the evening downing vintage beer and discussing the evidence in the Lakeside Vampire case. They traded some new thoughts each had on the case. The end of the night brought them no definite conclusions, but both felt the fog surrounding the case was starting to slowly dissipate.

Arriving at the lab the following morning, Drone could hardly contain himself. He called over his most compulsive technician, Joe Wahlkowski. Joe was known affectionately around the lab as Joe "The Wall", as once he started a job he wouldn't budge from it until he finished. Drone was told that one weekend, Joe had worked forty-eight consecutive hours to find a trace semen stain in a child abuse case. He ultimately found it, and as a result, was responsible for putting a pedophile behind bars for over a decade.

Drone called Joe into his office to explain the meticulous work that needed to be done. It would not be easy and the payoff a long shot.

"It might take days or longer, and it may be like chasing shadows," Drone admitted.

"I'll give it my best shot." Joe's word was his oath. That was all Drone needed to hear.

Ten miles away at the county courthouse, McKay was petitioning the court for an exhumation order on the last victim in the case, Mary Lou Halstead. In reviewing the photos, something he had seen had startled him. A Dr. Justin Marsone handled her autopsy. He was good, but still relatively new. McKay was in New Orleans attending the National Medical Examiner's conference when Halstead's body was discovered. Her autopsy was the only one in the entire Lakeside series that Dr. McKay had not personally quarterbacked.

Exhumations are a very touchy subject. Families hate them because it opens emotional wounds that have never fully closed. Law enforcement, and particularly the ME's office hate them because they imply something was "missed" the first time around. The press, on the other hand, loved them. A backhoe lifting freshly lain soil to hoist a casket from its "final" place of rest made for a great lead story on the six o'clock news. After calling in a few favors owed, McKay finally got the judicial okay to exhume the body of Mary Lou Halstead, the last and youngest victim of the Lakeside Vampire. It was scheduled for eight o'clock the following evening, after the Holy Sepulcher Cemetery was closed to the living for the night.

It was almost midnight at the DNA laboratory. Joe was running a second set of gas chromatography results on the samples he had been given. Several small peaks were showing up in each of the samples, in exactly the same spot. He looked at the printout again and again, first believing his imagination was getting overactive given the long days and late hour. He picked up a chemical reference book and leafed through pages to a large pullout chart. He ran his finger down and stopped when he came to what he had suspected he might find. His eyes widened in disbelief. He almost knocked over a chair as he leapt for the phone. He had no hesitation whatsoever to wake Drone at even this hour after what he had just discovered.

Evening had settled on Holy Sepulcher Cemetery. The low hum of machinery broke the otherwise serene atmosphere. The bright yellow Caterpillar backhoe finished unearthing the vault. A half an hour later the casket was hoisted out of the ground and several men moved it over to firm soil. A funeral director stood by and opened the coffin's lid. Using a bright portable lamp, Weston stared at Mary Lou's young, innocent face. Despite the trauma inflicted on the barely fifteen-year-old's body, she looked at peace. Her sky blue summer dress with small white daisy print looked more like a spring evening's casual attire than a burial garment. An unexpected feeling of sadness overcame McKay. He slowly studied each hand with a magnifying lens. After several minutes, he bent over with a skilled hand and retrieved a very small fragment of blonde hair entrapped deeply under the nail of her left index finger. He smiled as he noticed a portion of root bulb attached to the base of the hair. She had been a fighter. He placed the forceps in the evidence bag and instructed the crew to begin the re-interment.

Howard Ducray sat next to his fireplace and relaxed in his favorite chair with Sigmund lying beneath his feet. The dog snored and occasionally jerked his legs. Ducray was jealous of such a deep restful sleep. The fire burned not for warmth, but more for ambience. He liked things to be just right. He read the Sunday paper and dosed in and out of consciousness, his glass of Redwood Creek merlot slowly taking effect. He was startled awake by the sound of his phone ringing. It was almost eleven o'clock. His wife, Anna, had answered from the second floor of his home, and called down for him. He picked up the receiver and listened. The police chief was on the other end.

"My God, you're kidding me... how... yes... yes. I'll be there in thirty minutes."

Anna came downstairs looking puzzled. "Honey, what's going on, you look sick?"

"It's Otis Schenk. Apparently after evening showers he attacked one of the guards and knocked him unconscious. Then he took his gun and forced his way out of the building. They currently don't know where he is. Keep the doors and windows locked. Load my gun and put in on the nightstand. I'm not sure when I'll get back."

Back at the M.E.'s building McKay, Drone, and Wahlkowski gathered in the lab's main conference room. They had just heard on the news about Schenk's escape from the psychiatric hospital.

"What have you got?" McKay asked Drone impatiently.

"Joe finished running the last samples an hour ago. I reviewed the results, and I'm convinced those blood samples contained EDTA."

Weston's face dropped, "You're kidding me."

"Not a bit. We ran, re-ran and double-checked the results. Ethylenediaminetetraacetic acid, the versatile anticoagulant was present in the crime scene blood samples. Minute quantities, but definitely there," Drone added, almost not believing it himself.

"And you're sure it's not a contaminant?" McKay asked sounding like a defense attorney.

"I won't bore you with the scientific details but I am absolutely sure," Joe contributed.

"Then that means…" Weston's voice trailed off.

"That means that Otis Schenk was set up and someone planted his blood at the scene," Drone said finishing Weston's thought. Nobody in the room quite believed what the evidence was saying.

The police eventually tracked Otis Schenk to his mother's abandoned farmhouse out on route 20A. He was holed up inside and was believed to have access to significant firepower. A moment later a police cruiser pulled up with Dr. Ducray in the back seat. Police chief Jack Hammond came over to the car.

"Hello, Doc, we've had some very limited communication with him. He's already asked for you, but I think it's too risky. He seems only partially coherent, screaming that he's innocent of the murders. Quite a change of heart from the guy you said claimed his role in life was to be a human parasite," Hammond said as he un-holstered his service revolver. Hammond moved Ducray behind one of the police barricades. "It appears he's alone, and given the nature of his crimes, I don't think I'm going to take any chances with my men. I've already requested a police sniper be bought in. If he gets a clean shot, I'll give the order to take it," Hammond said firmly, determined not to add to Schenk's body count. "If we take him alive you can have a chat with him, but no way are you going into that house."

Back at the ME's office, McKay called a close friend at police headquarters and asked that a background check be done. The recently discovered laboratory evidence had him thinking about a new suspect in the Lakeside Murders, but he would need more information to support it. "Would you mind, Trudy, it really is important?"

"All right, but not a word to anyone. I'm not losing my pension with only eighteen months to go."

"You're a sweetheart. Call me when you get something."

"I will and you'll owe me one McKay."

Weston hung up and joined the others in the conference room.

"Well, what do we do know?" Joe asked.

"We wait," McKay answered.

A helicopter flew over the remote farmhouse shining a large floodlight on the dilapidated dwelling and surrounding grounds. A green van pulled up and stopped abruptly behind police lines. The back door opened and out stepped Frank Castleman, and ex-military sniper dressed in camouflage and carrying a 7.62 mm PSG-1 sniper rifle with a 3x9 power variable night vision scope. He looked around, scented the air, and seemed thrilled with the situation. He looked at Ducray and Hammond.

"God forgive me, but I love this. Chance to take out a scumbag like this really makes getting up in the morning worth it!" he said. Moments later he had himself situated in a large Elm tree thirty yards east of the house. He made himself comfortable in a makeshift prone position, turned on his scope, and chambered a round.

After thirty minutes, McKay received the phone call he'd been waiting for.

"Lucky for you, no one is ever around here on the night shift," said Trudy. "It's a very interesting file. Half a dozen foster homes, a couple of delinquency charges, animal cruelty, paramilitary affiliations and the like. How in the world did someone like this get a healthcare license?" she asked, thinking fearfully about her next office visit.

"Are you kidding me? You can do some scary stuff in this day and age with such easy access to the internet, hackers and identity theft. If you're bright enough, or demented enough, you wouldn't believe what you could do, or make it look like you've done," McKay said as his heart raced with the news.

"Hope that helps, Weston."

"More than you can imagine, Trudy." McKay hung up and called over to Joe. "Get Ducray on his pager, STAT. We've got to end this game now!"

Ducray's pager was barely audible over the noise of the loudspeaker, car engines, and helicopter overhead the old farmhouse. He recognized the number as the Medical Examiner's office and grabbed his cell phone and immediately started dialing.

"Hello, hello, Weston? It's Howard."

"Jesus, Howard what's all that noise?" Ducray took a moment to explain the situation, where he was, and why. Hearing this made McKay's heart pound.

"Howard, listen to me. Don't let them take Schenk out, do you hear me?"

"Weston, what are you talking about?"

"Just stop them! Schenk is not the Lakeside vampire. I said not. You have to trust me on this one. Do whatever it takes to get the police to back off!"

Twenty miles away in an upper class subdivision, the police quietly approached a two-story, brick colonial on Harcroft Drive. There was a quick knock on the door, but no one answered. Two officers grabbed the steel battering ram and began smashing in the front door. Two other officers clad in helmets and Kevlar vests barreled into the foyer of the home with their 9mm Glocks drawn and ready. A shadowy figure ran across an upstairs walkway.

"Freeze, it's the police, come down with your hands in the air. Do it now!" A shot from a high-power rifle rang out hitting the lead officer in the middle of his vest. A barrage of return shots were fired, and then the house became silent. The officers cautiously climbed the stairs and found the suspect lying dead with both legs sticking out into the hallway and the rest of the body lying still, just inside a small bedroom. Upon a thorough search of the house, the officers found an arsenal of weapons, military paraphernalia, and even a grenade launcher.

Shortly after, the Medical Examiner's steel blue Yukon arrived with Weston McKay exiting the vehicle as it rolled to a stop. He raced through the broken front door and up the stairs to the now lifeless body. He took quick mental note of the body's position, then rolled the corpse over. The empty, blank look of Franklin Beauregard stared vacantly at the ceiling. The blonde hair matted with blood from a single gunshot wound that had connected with his left temple in the deadly exchange.

The next morning, Dr. Ducray entered his office to see Weston McKay relaxing in his favorite chair.

"Well, Weston, have you decided to leave pathology for the more dignified life of a psychiatrist, yet?"

"Sorry, not a chance in hell, Howard! I just stopped by to tie up a few loose ends and to say hello."

"How can I help?"

"How well did you know Beauregard?"

"He'd worked for us at the clinic for almost two years now. I didn't really know him that well, but he always seemed pleasant and certainly very competent. However, it's well known that sociopathic personalities can be very charming if it suits their purposes."

"Well, apparently he took the samples he drew from Schenk during routine blood work. He then proceeded to plant Schenk's blood at the murder scenes. When Drone finally detected the EDTA in the samples, we were tipped off that those samples came from blood that had been collected with an anticoagulant, and not from an injury. Where he got the semen, though, remains a mystery to me."

"Maybe I can help with that one," Ducray said. "I spoke with Schenk at length yesterday. He's more coherent since being on his medication. Apparently Beauregard was giving Schenk a placebo instead of his anti-psychotic medications. When he got delusional, Beauregard took him to visit a prostitute, then collected the discarded condom. Beauregard came damn close to sending Schenk to the chair in place of himself, or at least lifelong incarceration in a psychiatric center. He's doing even better than I had hoped he would, since taking his real medication this past week."

"I'm glad to hear it."

"Yeah, Beauregard had convinced him that he was the killer, and with his deteriorating state of mind, Schenk consumed the idea and actually believed it. Given Schenk's deeply rooted need for recognition, of any sorts, and his delusional state, Schenk made an easy target for Beauregard.

Weston added, "By the way, the DNA from the hair I found on Mary Lou Halstead at the exhumation are a perfect match to Beauregard's. That should tie him firmly to at least one of the victims."

Weston pulled into his reserved parking space at the ME's office. Ed and Joe, who had been waiting for McKay to return, walked to his car smiling.

"Hey my man, don't even think about getting out! You're buying the drinks at One Eyed Jack's," Drone said with humor in his voice.

"Hey, why am I always buying?"

"Cause you're the man, Weston," Joe said as he helped himself into the rear seat of the Yukon.

"You're right, I am the man!" Weston replied with a touch of sarcasm as he smiled thinking of Big Mike and a cold Czech Pilsner. He closed his door and turned up the radio, which was ironically playing AC/DC's *Highway to Hell*.

Otis Schenk gradually edged closer to behaving normally. He religiously took the daily medications he was given. He certainly wanted to get well so he could get out of there. He had heard the whispers about Franklin Beauregard among the staff. He knew a secret about Franklin, but it wasn't what everyone thought. Franklin was a ranking member of a secret civilian militia that held some radical beliefs on personal freedom and limiting the government's role in an individual's life. Schenk knew Beauregard would never stand for the police barging into his house, not without a fight. He'd rather die than let the police enter his home. Beauregard's personal arsenal attested to that. Schenk had also counted on how very smart Ducray, McKay, and the others would be. How meticulous and detailed an investigation they would carry out. As he thought about how he drew tubes of his own blood and retrieved a few of Beauregard's hairs from a comb he left lying around the clinic, he smiled. He slowly ran his tongue along his sharply pointed teeth, drawing a small drop of blood, which he savored. If he kept getting better, and he would, he'd be out in less than a month. That was a good thing because he really felt the need for a nice warm drink.

STOLEN COLORS

My nerves were raw. It wasn't the most opportune time to take inventory of my situation but I didn't have much choice. I was in a rat-hole motel somewhere in Connecticut about a hundred miles from Boston. Jimmy was lying in the corner moaning and incoherent, having taken a shot to his lower chest earlier in the day. There was a painting thrown in the closet done by a guy who died unexpectedly at age forty-three. I had my .40 caliber Beretta sitting on the cheap faux oak veneer nightstand with three clips of ammunition stuffed in my pocket. The motel clerk was tied up on one of the twin beds with his mouth taped shut and there were probably half a dozen state troopers within a thirty-mile radius of me. These were, however, the least of my problems. It was Victor Scarpesi's crew that made my blood freeze. How close they were, I had no idea. Admittedly, things could have been better, but they weren't all bad. That painting I mentioned is by a fella named Johann... as in Johann Vermeer... and it's worth at least twenty million dollars. That isn't bad money for a small antiques dealer and ex con from upstate New York.

If I really think about it, this whole thing started in Boston in March of 1990. A couple of art thieves dressed as Boston cops talked their way into the Isabella Steward Gardner Museum, tied up the security guards, and walked off with a dozen masterpieces worth over three hundred million dollars. If you don't believe me look it up on the internet, every word of it is true. The one Vermeer in the collection is entitled *The Concert*. Now Delft's famous son's painting was stashed in the cramped closet of a forty-dollar per night, fleabag motel called the Queen's Court.

I took off my black sweatshirt and loosened the laces on my rubber-soled shoes. I removed the wig and fake facial hair I was wearing. I casually lit up one of my Marlboros and watched Jimmy finally die through the mist of blue smoke I blew into the air. I felt bad, but there wasn't a hell of a lot I could do about it. His last words were "Han... Han..." and what they meant at the time, I didn't have a clue. That would take some time to figure out. So for now it was just me, Johann, and the motel clerk whose nametag simply read, *Hello, I'm Carl. Ask me how I can help.* Well, Carl, for starters you can figure out how to get me the hell out of Connecticut without ending up in jail, or worse, if Scarpesi finds me, a shallow grave. Once that's done, how about hooking me up with the painting's buyer, a retired international shipping mogul who has promised a substantial sum for this portrait. I'm sure it would add to his personal enjoyment as the centerpiece of his four million-dollar island estate off the coast of Greece. After that Carl, help me establish a new identity in the Cayman Islands so that I can live happily ever after in my million-dollar beachfront bungalow. My only worries will be the quality of exotic drinks I'll be sipping and the size of the Tarpon and Sailfish I'll be catching off my forty-foot luxury yacht. Yes, Carl, that's how you can help. Think you're up to it? I looked out the window and down in the valley. I saw the flashing red lights of a trooper's car as it sped down interstate 66. The sharks smelled blood in the water. I had to think fast and move even faster.

I put my Beretta against Carl's head and slowly took the tape off his mouth. I told him, "Listen, my friend. You are going to make a phone call to whoever owns this hell hole and tell them

102

you're not feeling well and need someone to replace you. Not having a clerk up front is eventually going to arouse somebody's suspicion and we don't want that."

"Yes… yes, I will do whatever you want… please don't hurt me," he stammered looking sufficiently scared to cooperate.

"No screw ups or you'll be joining Jimmy over there in the happy ever after, got it?" I said, giving him a clear view of the gun's barrel.

"No… no screw ups… I promise, none," he said his eyes wide and hands shaking. He made the call and came up with a bullshit story about a bad case of diarrhea and having to leave immediately. Another clerk would be there in half an hour. I doubt they'll lose much business given the quality of the rooms and the less than desirable location. Thunder pounded the sky and it started raining hard enough to start the ceiling leaking like a burst water pipe. It was the perfect ending to a wonderful day. Torrential downpour or not, I wasn't planning to stick around much longer. I packed up Johann's painting, slid the Beretta in my belt and told Carl we were going for a little ride.

I put Jimmy's body in the bathtub and after wiping down the room of prints and changing the license plates on Carl's spiffy green Toyota Corolla we slipped onto a back road leading towards Massachusetts. It was ten a.m. and Carl's family wouldn't miss him for at least five hours; by that time, we'd have ourselves situated in Boston. Everything was going well until the remote road we were traveling on flooded. There was what looked like an abandoned farmhouse a few miles back. I told Carl to turn the car around and we backtracked and arrived at the rickety old house a few minutes later. I had Carl pull the car in the back, far out of sight. I spent a few minutes checking out the place as best as I could in the darkness. It wasn't the Hilton, but It would have to do until the road was open, which given the continued downpour, wasn't going to be anytime soon. I tied Carl's hands behind his back and told him to get some sleep. I should have taped his mouth shut because for the next half an hour he wouldn't shut up. I finally threatened to shoot him before he finally closed his trap and went to sleep. Wouldn't you know it he snored like a truck driver. It didn't' make much difference, given my adrenaline level I wasn't seeing any Z's anytime soon. I lay down and looked around. The sun was visible as the clouds dissipated. The place looked better in the light. It was probably quite a spread in its day. Natural wood planked floors and big external oak beam rafters with a step down family room. I might have retired to a place like this... that is if Jimmy Calahan hadn't waked into my life six months ago. It's a day I won't ever forget.

I was putting up a display of early nineteenth century parisian monocular microscopes when he walked into my shop. He browsed around for five minutes or so, then seeing me alone approached.

"Mr. Zinser... Robert Zinser?" he inquired. I looked up to see a tall, powerful looking man wearing a gray tailored silk suit and carrying a black leather briefcase. His hair was thick and short and he spoke with a Boston accent. His tortoise shell glasses perfectly circled his steel gray eyes.

"Yes, I'm Bob Zinser, how can I help you?"

"Well, I was wondering if we could have lunch tomorrow. I've got a proposal with significant financial implications and would like to discuss it in private with you," he said, as he handed me his business card. It stated he was an art authenticator who had trained at the Sorbonne in France and held a master's degree in classical studies and antiques.

I looked at my appointment schedule and was able to meet with him at one o'clock. He was pleased, gave me the name of the restaurant and told me he would see me tomorrow. An instant later he vanished down Beuning Boulevard. I occasionally had distributors approach me with a lot or two of antiques they needed to unload so I didn't think much about the meeting. Business had sagged with the economy and I certainly was grateful for any business opportunities that arose.

At exactly one o'clock I walked into the Hillcrest Family Restaurant in downtown Angola, a small upstate New York town about ten miles from my shop. It was a crisp, sunny November morning. I saw Jimmy sitting in a corner booth perusing a large, dirty laminated menu and walked over to join him.

"Hello, Jimmy," I said taking a seat.

"Afternoon, Bob. How are things today? And before there is any argument, I'm buying lunch today."

"All right." We ordered coffee and began to talk.

"Listen Bob, I know about your past and that's why I'm here." I looked up surprised but didn't say a word. "You had the reputation as one of the best cat burglars that ever—"

"Wait a second," I interrupted, "that was a long time ago. I did five long years for that and I'm not planning any return trips." I got up to leave.

"It's worth half a million for one job, and I'll absolutely guarantee the victim won't say a word to the police," he said talking to the menu. I sat back down, swallowed a mouthful of strong, bad coffee and somewhat reluctantly told him to go on. It turned out that a rare Vermeer painting that was stolen from the Isabella Gardner Museum over a decade ago was in the possession of a wealthy underworld figure named Victor Scarpesi. He controlled organized crime in Western New York, including the area where I lived. He had a mansion on the lake where Jimmy said the painting was housed. Apparently Jimmy knew a very wealthy Greek who would pay quite a sum of money for the painting, and now Calahan just needed someone crazy enough to steal it for him. He offered me a hundred thousand in advance with the rest payable on delivery of the painting. That was a good chunk of my retirement money all made in a day's work. Actually it was more like six weeks if you count all the planning, scouting and preparation it would take. Still, it was damn good money, not to mention tax free. I did quite a bit of soul searching and finally, I'm not ashamed to admit, greed got the best of me. I called Jimmy back a week later and told him I'd take the job.

I surveyed Scarpesi's house for two weeks. The place was gorgeous. Over six-thousand square feet, seven bedrooms, five bathrooms and a fully equipped chef's kitchen with top of the line Viking appliances. Three fire places and a fully equipped movie theater. No scrimping here. Now about getting in... the main obstacles were two aggressive German shepherds that patrolled the gated property and an alarm system wired to the house. The security seemed average, especially given the value of the painting and the notoriety of the owner. Time had made him comfortable and Scarpesi had significantly let down his guard. Jimmy was right about another thing, his reporting a stolen painting was not an option. Of course Scarpesi didn't really need the police it would be much easier just to have whoever stole the painting killed. Justice would be harsh and quick, much more so than any American court system could deliver. A deep well or an unmarked grave in the Adirondacks awaited any who crossed this capo di capos. It certainly had happened to others.

Finally the time had come. We had waited until Scarpesi was in Florida for Christmas. He left one bodyguard at the house. Using remote electrical rewiring, I purposely tripped the alarm after midnight. As expected the police were there in ten minutes and found nothing. Faulty alarm. I did this again at two a.m. and four a.m. for the next two nights, producing the same results. As anticipated on the fourth night, the estate's occupant did not arm the alarm system, choosing a good night's sleep over safety. That left only dealing with the dogs. A few pounds of sausage containing a powerful tranquilizer provided the simplest solution.

Somehow Jimmy knew the painting was hung in a private reading room located in the subbasement connected to a separate alarm system. I entered through a side door, which led to the garage. It took less than five minutes to remove the deadbolt and once inside I had the leisure to open the second door into the house, the garage provided adequate cover from any passing traffic. I checked my watch. It was one-twenty-eight in the morning, by one-thirty-six I was in the kitchen and heading down to the basement. Halfway down I stopped dead in my tracks. I heard footsteps upstairs. I only took a breath when I heard the toilet flush. I waited a full fifteen minutes before I took another step. The only sound was my heart pounding in my chest. I pulled a heavy metal latch that opened a four foot square section of the floor, and descended six metal steps to the foyer of the subbasement. An oak door marked the entryway into the reading room. A red eye flickered above from the corner of the room indicating an internal alarm was activated. I followed the wire up along the basement wall and located the security box. Within a few minutes I managed to disable the alarm and was again standing in front of the oak door, the last barricade separating me from the painting.

I was amazed at how quickly the lock gave way, especially given the value of what lay beyond the threshold. I slowly opened the door, every one of my senses in overdrive. I turned the flashlight to the far wall and stopped cold. Vermeer's painting hung over an Italian carved marble fireplace. Scarpesi might be a hoodlum, but the man obviously had class. A vaulted stained glass dome capped the expansive cherry bookshelves, which were filled with hundreds of leather bound books. The executive desk and impeccable red leather furniture completed the ambiance of the room. The Vermeer, one of less than a dozen known to exist, complemented the room perfectly. I wished I had more time to enjoy the atmosphere but I needed to get moving. I wrapped the painting in a canvas satchel and started climbing the stairs. According to plan, Jimmy should be pulling in front of the house in a few minutes and he would pay me the balance and be on his way to Boston with the Vermeer. There a representative of the painting's soon to be new owner waited. I made my way towards the front door when I heard the unsettling sound of a shotgun shell being chambered.

"Who the hell are you?" A voice echoed in the darkness. Before I had a chance to answer, the front door burst open and Jimmy fired a round into the threatening figure. He flinched, pointing the shotgun at Jimmy and fired before falling to the floor. I swung the canvas satchel with the painting over my shoulder and half carried and half dragged Jimmy into the stolen Lincoln Towne Car. A second shotgun blast sent a flurry of pellets into the side window as I slammed down on the accelerator and drove out of sight.

"Almost perfect, too bad that guy's got a bladder problem," I said trying to lighten up the rather tense situation.

"Forget about that, you gotta get us to Boston. I'll throw in another hundred grand for taxi fare. I've got a meeting with one of Theropoulus' representatives tomorrow night," he said between grunts. He breathing became deeper and slower.

"You just relax. We'll have to change cars soon." I left on the disguise Jimmy had given me earlier that day. It made me look ten years older. "Scarpesi's people will be on the hunt shortly, if they aren't already," I said as I scoured the road for a new ride. We found a nice Subaru Outback parked on a quiet side street. I switched plates with another car and in ten minutes we were on our way to Boston. We took a meandering route to keep from being predictable to our pursuers. Jimmy wasn't looking so good and I tried to talk him into going to a hospital. He refused. The only concession I got from him was stopping at a motel to get him cleaned up and have a better look at his chest wound. It looked like a major storm was coming as I pulled into the Queen's Court, a real flophouse-looking motel in broken down neighborhood in Connecticut. I could tell community revitalization wasn't on anybody's radar screen for this hellhole. I pulled around back to keep Jimmy out of site then went to the register. The motel clerk, Carl, did the paperwork and as I started to leave, he quipped,

"Hey man, did you just kill somebody?" I looked down and hadn't realized that my shirt and coat were stained with Jimmy's blood. I couldn't take any chances so I stepped back to the counter and stuck my Beretta in Carl's face.

"No, but it's still an option my friend," I said motioning with the Beretta for him to follow me. I made him turn on the "No Vacancy" sign and walked him over to the room. After he was bound and gagged, I helped Jimmy into the room. I explained to Jimmy what happened, and tossed the painting in the closet. Jimmy wasn't looking any better. His eyes had a vacant stare and he was mumbling. He said something about his wife… and then mumbled, "Han." I put the gun on the nightstand and took off my coat. I lit up a cigarette and then wondered what the hell I was going to do. After Jimmy died I eventually ended up in this abandoned farmhouse sheltering from the storm surging around me.

The farmhouse was damp and cold. I must have finally dozed off for a half an hour or so. At some point it had stopped raining. Carl was still snoring away, being oblivious to one's predicament is a blessing of youth. Before waking him up, I went out to the car and looked through Jimmy's briefcase. My four hundred thousand was there. I had a feeling that was a pittance compared to what was coming. Written on the back of his business card there was the word *Theropoulus*, as well as a location and a time, today at five o'clock. A separate piece of paper had the name Han Van Meegeren with a smiley face drawn next to it. I had no idea what that meant.

I roused Carl out of his slumber and left him haunch tied as I settled him into the back seat. It was two p.m., still plenty of time to get to the meeting. Using an assumed name I checked into a small motel ten miles from the scheduled meeting place in front of Martin's Seafood Restaurant in Quincy Market. I secured Carl in the bathroom and went out to ditch the car in a large parking lot. I then caught a cab to Hertz and rented a Ford Taurus, which I drove back to the motel. I had picked up some food on the way and Carl and I feasted on steak hoagies, Pepsi, and apple pie.

"Carl, I have a proposition for you."

"Anything has to be better than this," he said with a touch of humor I didn't expect from someone who had been kidnapped and dragged over a hundred miles from his place of employment.

"My work is almost done. I need to deliver some merchandise to a man I'll meet in Quincy Market. You make the exchange for me and then develop a bad case of amnesia. If you cooperate, you get an envelope with one hundred fifty thousand dollars. If you don't, one of my associates will pay you a visit in the near future and bury you, probably alive, in very, very remote part of the national park."

"Money sounds fine." Carl had suddenly become a man of few words.

I pulled into the market and parked about forty yards from the restaurant, adjacent to an outdoor pastry café. I pointed to a bench and gave Carl the satchel containing the painting. I sat back with my Tasco field binoculars and watched. A man dressed like a tourist carrying a camera and large grocery bag walked up to Carl and sat down. He began eating an apple for several minutes, then got up taking the satchel and leaving the paper bag. Carl retrieved the bag and walked slowly towards the car, just as I instructed. Once inside, he took a deep breath. He was visibly upset. I could see that the recent events had finally gotten to him.

I opened Jimmy's briefcase and slowly counted out one hundred fifty thousand dollars. If nothing else, both with promises and threats, I was a man of my word. I drove him back to the parking lot where I had ditched his car and said goodbye. All in all, he wasn't bad company. I'd thought I'd probably miss him just a little on the ride back to New York. I drove a few miles and stopped. I looked at the large brown bag and slowly picked it up feeling the weight in my hands. I unfolded the top and looked inside. I began counting and counting. One and a half million dollars and a note saying the balance would be paid once a scientific authentication of the painting was complete. There was a contact number and code name for Jimmy to call in thirty days. Because of the large sum of money, the balance would be transferred to an overseas account that Jimmy was to provide at the time of the next contact. I guessed given the circumstances, Mr. Theropoulus, or whatever his real name was, got himself one hell of a deal on the painting.

I took the Amtrak train back to New York and removed the closed sign from my storefront window. I picked up a copy of the Times and the Boston Globe. I immediately turned to the obituaries. There he was, picture and full spread article. Mr. James Calahan. Died unexpectedly. Loving husband of... professor of art history and antiquities, Boston University... renowned art authenticator... author of several books including an internationally acclaimed scholarly work on the twentieth century's greatest art forger... Han Van Meegeren, the famed Vermeer forger who had duped several world-renowned art experts in the nineteen thirties and forties.

In the quite town of Newton, Massachusetts, the recently widowed and extremely distraught Eleanor Calahan wept. Her cousin Marion and husband Jack came up from Virginia to help her get things in order in preparation for selling her home. Eleanor was of little help, and the burden fell on Marion and Jack to arrange the large estate sale. It was a rushed affair and Eleanor just wanted it done and to get away as soon as possible. Jimmy's belongings were packed, thrown away or put out for sale. As Marion cleaned out the basement she found an old box behind a false wall. She looked inside and was surprised to find a Boston policeman's uniform complete with badge and shoes. She wondered if it was an old Halloween costume. She slapped a thirty-dollar tag on it and placed the box on one of a dozen tables littering the front lawn of the house.

It wasn't until Mrs. Meyers, the curmudgeonly recluse from Braintree, got home and unpacked the uniform that she noticed a second layer to the box. She thought how crafty she had been talking down the price to only twenty dollars. She planned to cut up the uniform and use it for patches. She pulled up the fake bottom of the container and noticed a rolled up painting. Her eyes were not good but it appeared to be of three people, one of them playing a piano. She didn't have room in her house for another painting and thought she would toss it out with Friday's trash. However, even to her bad eyes, the painting seemed different than anything she had seen. She decided to hang it in her bedroom next to a sketch of her long dead husband. It didn't matter that it looked in need of a good cleaning, she rarely had visitors and more than likely she would be the only one to ever see it.

A month later I was cruising down the Atlantic seaboard. "Hey Ernesto! What are you doing to me? This Daiquiri is short on both strawberries and rum. What am I paying you for? And when do we dock at Nantucket? I've got a seven o'clock dinner reservation at The Mad Hatter's. Don't forget to fill the auxiliary tanks once we're there. Next week, I think I'll make that stop in the Keys I was talking about," I said while lighting up a Montecristo Mini Belicoso and feeling the cool ocean breeze blowing across the bow of my yacht affectionately named *Jimmy's Secret*.

MYSTERY COVE

My mind drifted as I drove along back roads that ran parallel to an isolated stretch of the interstate, passing through identical looking small towns where gas was still pumped by attendants and soda was served in glass bottles. Men with tattered clothes and unkempt beards sipped cheap beer on the porches of their double-wide trailers, laughing at jokes only they could understand. The hum of the engine and the monotonous scenery allowed my past to slowly drift into my consciousness, almost imperceptible at first, but before I knew it, eventually commanding my complete attention. The words haunted me. They said if anyone betrayed their trust they would "never get out of the agency alive." Apparently the brass isn't as smart as they'd like to think. I am indeed out, and currently very much alive. To bolster my security, I slid my right hand along my leg stopping at the Glock 9mm secured in a custom made ankle holster. I gazed over at Maria, my wife of just three months, who had fallen asleep and was softly breathing with her head against the padded door of our convertible Mercedes. I snaked the car along a particularly lonely stretch of road, crossing the Mannamuska Creek on a rickety wooden bridge that was so narrow it allowed passage of only one vehicle at a time. From this point I'd probably be at our new house in less than twenty minutes. I was getting bored with the one radio station I could pick up. It was mostly static anyway. I liked the isolation but this was getting to be a bit much. Hoping for some conversation, I gave Maria a gentle shake and she slowly opened her eyes.

"Hey, are we there yet?" she said barely opening her eyes.

"No, not quite hun, but shortly."

"And I'm still not sleeping because ..." she mumbled in her French accent.

"I couldn't go another minute without hearing your angelic voice," I said with a restrained laugh.

"Yeah, Roger, you're so full of..."

At that moment the car swerved as I missed clipping a deer that had bolted from behind a thick row of yellow birch trees. I brought the car to a halt near a small abandoned cemetery. The gravestones looked unattended and the iron gate was long rusted. A sign hung on an angle and read *Hillcrest Memorial Grounds*. At that moment, I was thankful not to be joining the patrons.

"Whoa, that was close," I said my heart still pounding, "aren't you glad you were awake to see that?" Maria glared at me, looking startled as well.

"Can we just get there in one piece? If we get in an accident out here, no one will find us for days. It's nice to get away, but I think we're pushing it out here, Mister Davie Crockett!" I gently reminded her she was the one who found this house. I smiled at her and sped back onto the main road, feeling at peace for the first time in months.

The sun was setting on a crimson sky when we finally pulled up the gravel driveway. The wind began blowing hard causing the elm trees to rustle like a flock of startled birds. The clouds turned a dusky gray and hung heavily in the sky.

It took only a few minutes to unload the car. The house was musty and hadn't been occupied in several months. We opened the windows and pulled the dusty sheets off the furniture. Maria placed fresh floral patterned sheets on the beds while I stocked the refrigerator. I then slipped onto the back deck with a cold beer. I watched trout break water as they grabbed mayflies in a stream that slowly curved its way around the back side of the house. It was turning into a stormy cool July evening and I was content to be in the company of nature. In the distance I could see a dozen strawberry bushes bursting with plump red fruit. After swallowing the last of my imported ale, I walked back to the car and brought in my security case. It contained a Sig SG-550 .223 sniper rifle with mounted night vision optics. It also housed my Model 1300 Winchester Defender with an eight round magazine that I kept for any unexpected close quarter encounters and my trusted 7mm Remington Magnum. A half of a million in cash was carefully stashed beneath the weapons, behind the cubed foam padding that lined the case. The weapons attested to my prior line of work and the money; the reason I left it so abruptly.

The agency, more precisely the agency within the agency, promised to bury any renegades and by anyone's definition, I was just that. If they believed I was alive they would be relentless in their pursuit. Without question they would like to make an example of me. If they wanted a war, however, I was prepared to give them one. My only hope is that they considered me already dead, a trophy for some Afghani Warlord. I couldn't dwell on that, there was too much work to get done.

Within the hour I had set up my desktop computer and also had my laptop in working order. I headed to the fridge to grab another beverage. Thunder sounded in the distance and bolts of white lightning streaked across the sky illuminating the surrounding hills.

"Honey, are you coming upstairs?" I heard Maria call.

"On my way, with a beer in hand!"

"Well hurry up, I'm dehydrating, what's for dinner? Perhaps some La Buchette Charcutiere?"

"Not quite but close. After we down our brews, I'll clean up the grill, and roast some dogs. If I'm lucky, I'll have a few cooked before I get dumped on." Just then there was a short knock at the door. I was surprised, but not really alarmed. Agency reps wouldn't be so cordial as to use the front entrance.

"Hello, Roger? Maria... anybody home?" It was John Koplan, a neighbor that lived in the next house away, a quarter of a mile down the road. I opened the door to find him and his wife, Jessie. They were both in their early fifties, but looked younger than their years.

"Hi John, Jessie, come in, Maria is upstairs and should be down shortly," I said, happy to have the company. It seemed days had passed without seeing anyone but convenience store clerks and gas station attendants.

"Hope you don't mind us dropping by. We were on our way back from the grocery store and saw your lights were still on. Sorry about stopping in unannounced."

"No problem whatsoever," I said motioning them inside.

The Koplans were one of a handful of people who knew we had this house. They had taken quickly to Maria and spent a lot of time showing her the area. After Maria picked it out, I bought the house with cash, using a fabricated identity. Being someone I wasn't, was one of the many skills I had acquired throughout my years in Uncle Sam's service. I planned to keep my new last name and the other particulars I had devised. I hoped that would help deter unannounced visits from former associates. I looked forward to a peaceful retirement in this remote lakeside town of Mystery Cove.

After a brief chat with our new neighbors, Maria and I bid them farewell, and headed upstairs to the loft. It was a large bedroom with antique cherry furniture and a mahogany four-poster point bed. The floorboards were solid oak planks and a large window overlooked the river. A small radio sat atop one of the handcrafted end tables and a green and red Persian rug sprawled across a good portion of the floor. We were both tired, but recent enough newlyweds that our carnal desires won out. It was near midnight when I noticed Maria finally drifted off.

I laid awake, my mind wandering over the past three years. It was the first time I wasn't on the move and had time to reflect. My mind drifted back to when I was a new recruit with the anti-terrorism coalition or ATC. It was an international group of fifty men broken down into mission groups of five. I had another American, two Brits, and a Belgian in my squad. The training was six months of absolute hell. Imagine Navy Seals cranked up a couple notches… brutal. Low level parachute drops in the middle of the night in the worst weather, hours floating in frigid water, hand to hand combat, days without food or sleep, and endless uphill marches in sand or mud. Weapon training was intense and covered everything from side arms to sidewinder missiles. Then there was the psychological stress. Days in solitary confinement, administration of psychoactive medications and the infamous missing weekend. We all experienced it. Forty-eight hours that just disappeared from our lives. We all remembered the IV lines being started, then complete blackness. Some of us recalled bits and pieces of what happened after that but it never made much sense. Broken visions of people talking, electric shocks, repetitive phrases, and sensory deprivation tanks. There were rumors of subliminal messages and attempts at subconscious mind control. None of us knew what to believe. We were all relieved when that part of the training was complete. Everyone agreed that it was the most disturbing aspect of the entire military training experience

Within six weeks of completing the program I found myself on the Afghanistan-Pakistan boarder, in an area known as Angor Adda. There, my group lived like rats in a cave. Our job was to disrupt any attempts by the Taliban to regroup and to track down any terrorist cells forming in the area. For obvious reasons we would never be recognized for our efforts but a few of our successes included aiding in the capture of Handi al-Ahdal, Muhammed Abdulah, Ansar al-Islam, and Abu Zarqani, as well as more than a dozen kills. We were trailing the big target and got close a few times but not quite close enough. Our work was ninety-five percent boredom and five percent absolute terror. Filthy, hard and dangerous sums it up pretty well. Not your father's war. Friends in that area were at times as likely to bury a knife in your back as any enemy.

It was during a late night raid in the village of Abba Kasal that my life took an unexpected turn. We had just killed several insurgents outside of an abandoned mosque. When we got inside we realized we had hit upon a heroin smuggling ring. Aside from packaged drugs there were two decaying wine barrels full of cash in several currencies, including a lot of U.S. greenbacks. Protocol meant turning both the heroin and money back to our C.O. I could tell by the look in the Belgian's eyes he had other intentions. His nostrils flared and he raised his weapon. Before I knew it his Uzi was spilling lead and blood, and the two Brits went down taken out from behind. I managed to fire one shot from my Glock before I felt me left upper thigh explode. Charlie Chambers, the other American in our group ended the exchange of gunfire by putting a bullet in the Belgian's neck. He hit the floor as a red puddle formed around his head. My left pant leg was darkened and sticky and I started getting lightheaded. Charlie stopped the bleeding with a tourniquet and constructed a makeshift splint for my left leg. No sooner had he finished when we spotted a group of rebels who came over the far foothills that were just east of us. He hoisted the contraband, as well as myself, into our Hummer and sped towards base camp.

"Can you believe that shit? That son of a bitch Belgian!" he shouted above the noise of the truck. "I hope they burn him and hang him in the town square."

"Never would have guessed it Charlie. I mean you train with someone for..." before I could finish I heard the desert air snap sharply and watched Charlie's head drop with a sniper's bullet in his right temple. The Hummer swerved violently to the left, then came to a rolling halt. I slid over the front seat reopening my leg wound. I groaned in pain and took a deep breath before going on. I situated Charlie's limp body to shield my own and moved into the driver's seat. I slammed on the accelerator as I heard the distinct crack of more shots being fired as bullets buzzed overhead. I was hoping these guys hadn't spent much time on the practice range, but as I looked at Charlie I doubted that was the case. I was in rough shape and felt terrible about not being able to check on the two Brits we'd left behind. I hoped they were already dead. I didn't want to imagine their fate if they ended up in the hands of one of the insurgent groups or anti-coalition villagers.

I stopped the Hummer when I thought it was safe. I looked over my shoulder at the cargo now sitting in the back seat. It's funny how a few months of heat, isolation, and being surrounded by death can change lifelong values so quickly. I decided to dump the drugs and then used every last bit of my strength to bury Charlie in a shallow grave. I abruptly turned the truck around and headed in the opposite direction. The months spent working counterintelligence had given me several contacts in the unpatrolled border areas. Some were friendly to Americans, and the rest could be bribed. When you become a renegade there is a time you cross a line and you know you're never going back. That point isn't always clear at that particular moment, but you can feel it in your gut. I was there.

I became increasingly uneasy as the days passed, the admonitions of my chief instructor grabbing my attention at unexpected times. We were an elite group he said, and any abdication of our duty would be met with the harshest retribution. Our guilt, he stated, would make us our own worst enemies. We would regret betraying our sacred trust. The agency had tentacles that reached into any hole we thought we could hide. In order to keep my sanity I lived on the assumption they considered me KIA, my body just never recovered. Just in case, however, I kept enough firepower to help me sleep at night.

It had taken me six months to build an alias and make it back into The States. It was another six before I completely established my identity as Roger Hammersmith, formerly one Roger Halstead. Then there was Maria, the first semblance of decency since these events transpired. She unexpectedly came up and introduced herself as I dined alone at a trendy Manhattan restaurant. She was long, lean and had a French accent to add to the package. We had many of the same interests in art and music and after a whirlwind romance we married in a private ceremony six months after we first met. I convinced her to move to a secluded area with me, explaining I had inherited a large sum of money. Calling it an inheritance, however, veered widely from the truth. I had over two million dollars in an offshore account in the Cayman Islands plus the half a million cash in my immediate possession. I talked her into spending six months in a remote waterfront town and six months of travel to exotic destinations. We talked about Aruba, Buenos Aires and various European destinations. We both hoped someday to walk the Great Wall of China. She gladly gave up her stressful job as a Wall Street analyst for the life I had to offer. Her mystical appearance in my life signaled that the hard times were over.

I looked up at the clock to see that it was well past two a.m. when I finished rehashing the last three years of my life. I definitely had some demons to exorcise and consciously thinking about it was at least a start. I eventually fell into a deep sleep and didn't awake until I smelled the bacon and eggs cooking. The aroma of freshly brewed coffee hung in the air. I was famished. It was nearly nine o'clock. I hadn't slept this late in months. I jumped out of bed and headed downstairs.

"Good morning," Maria said as she turned over several sizzling strips of bacon.

"Hey babe, I didn't know you could cook."

"There's a lot you don't know about me! You want juice with your breakfast? It's fresh squeezed."

"Affirmative!" I gave her a hug and kissed the back of her neck. I then slid into my executive chair and booted up the computer. I had six e-mail messages waiting since last evening. Four were spam, one a receipt from an internet purchase, and one whose subject line simply read "IT'S OVER". Out of curiosity I opened the message half expecting to see an advertisement for Viagra, Xanax, or Valium at half price. Or perhaps another offer for an herbal penis enlarger guaranteed to make me a better lover. Instead it read simply, "Your worst enemy is here. More information will follow." I swallowed hard and felt my body tense. Given my particular circumstances I had to be concerned. In the end I chalked it up to prank mail and tried not to let it bother me, although that really wasn't possible. I decided to wait and see what happened next.

Maria spent the next few days tilling an area for a vegetable garden while I did some touch up painting and replaced several of the window screens. There were several hornets' nests to dispose of and we needed a new sump pump. The fireplace was black with soot and the basement was still a mess. I decided to take the ten-mile ride into town to pick up some lawn tools, a hose, a few mousetraps, and an extension cord. When I arrived back home I saw John and Jessie's Subaru Forrester parked in front, so I parked out on the road. I walked around the side of the house to attach the new hose and heard them talking as I stood outside the kitchen window. Without realizing it, my old instincts took over and I started eavesdropping.

"So when you going to do it?" It was John's voice.

"Soon, I don't know exactly when, but it will have to be soon," Maria answered.

"Does he suspect anything?" asked Jessie.

"I doubt it; he's been so busy around here. I think his guard is down."

"Do you need our help?" John offered.

"No, I can take care of things myself," Maria said confidently.

"You know we're available if you need us," Jessie urged.

"Thanks, Jessie but I think I can take care of it myself. I've been thinking about the details for a few days now. I need some more information before I decide which way to go about it."

"All right, John and I need to be getting back home. If you decide you want any help, be sure to call us."

"I will. I'll be cautious. I have to be absolutely certain that he has no idea what's going on. I've noticed he's been acting a bit paranoid lately."

I heard John and Jessie get up to leave and I immediately jumped up and rounded to the front of the house as though I was just approaching.

"Hi there Roger. We were just visiting with Maria," John said as he closed the front door.

"Hello neighbors, how's life treating you?" I said placing my recent purchases on the front porch.

"Can't complain. Have to pick tomatoes and strawberries this afternoon, but right now I've got to get Jessie to town," John said as he slipped into his windbreaker.

"I've got an appointment with Dr. Glover the ophthalmologist. I might need cataract surgery," Jessie explained.

"Well, I hope it all goes well and don't feel bad if you have to drop off a few quarts of strawberries. Strawberry shortcake is a favorite dessert of mine. Especially with homemade whipped cream," I said acting nonchalant. As John bent down to tie his shoe I noticed the .38 he was carrying in the small of his back.

"We'll be sure you get some. Well we need to be going. Enjoy this beautiful day," John said as he took Jessie's arm and walked towards their car.

"Will do."

I went inside and heard Maria already getting in the shower. I walked up the stairs and down the hallway to the bathroom door. I opened it and saw her shaving her long legs, looking not unlike a flamingo from a south Florida game preserve.

"Hey there. I just saw John and Jessie leaving."

"Yeah, they stopped by for coffee. John had some leftover mulch and wondered if we could use any."

"What were you all talking about?" I asked casually.

"Their grandkids. And Jessie and I exchanged a few recipes. She gave me tips on fertilizing as well. She's a real encyclopedia on gardening."

"I couldn't help but overhear. Sounds as though you have something planned for me," I said, my voice now getting an edge.

"No, nothing."

"Don't lie to me Maria, what the hell is going on?" I was now yelling and growing increasingly agitated.

"Roger, nothing is going on," she said as she began rinsing off the shaving cream. I reached in, grabbed her arm and squeezed. I looked directly into her eyes. "I said, what's going on?"

"Jesus Roger, are you crazy?" I squeezed harder and just stared at her. "All right, I was planning a surprise thirty-fifth birthday party for you. In case you've forgotten, your birthday is in two weeks. Are you happy now? You've ruined the surprise." I let go of her arm and could clearly see my finger imprints in her flesh.

"I'm sorry… I… I'm really sorry, honey… I mean… I thought..."

Maria was visibly upset. She wiped tears from her eyes.

"You're scaring me Roger. You've seemed on the edge lately. Is something going on? I really think we need to talk about this."

"No… just a lot of old memories coming back. Someday I'll tell you all about them, I promise." I apologized again and walked downstairs. The thought of John carrying that gun still bothered me. He didn't seem the NRA type. Maybe I was just being paranoid. I turned on the computer and checked my email. There was a message from the same nondescript address, someone_187@hotmail.com with a subject again reading, "IT'S OVER". The message was succinct and said,

I am closer than you think.

I will give you proof shortly.

You have a debt to repay.

Thoughts raced through my head. Someone knew about the money and wanted some or all of it and would probably stop at nothing to get it. But who? Anybody who knew the details was already dead. It couldn't be the agency. They wouldn't play games and drag this out. A quick bullet in the head as I pumped gas, or my car exploding after turning the key was their M.O. Maybe they're purposely trying to make me suffer. No… no… it has to be the money. Somebody wants a cut. I didn't have much hope in tracking down the location of the e-mail messages. I'm sure it was strategically routed between several different servers before it got to me. But still, I had a few computer tricks I wanted to employ before totally giving up. I needed to get away for a moment. I took a short walk out back. When I returned, I decided to grab the mail. When I opened the box my stomach dropped. There, placed neatly on the top of a stack of letters was an unspent 7mm Remington magnum cartridge. The son of a bitch was in town. I didn't touch a thing. I went inside and called the sheriff, and then I went to the basement to retrieve my shotgun.

Sheriff Frank Masters was well over six feet tall, thin with closely cropped jet-black hair. He was from a family who had lived in this area for over seven generations. I gave him some, but not all, of the details about what had happened. I mostly wanted the bullet checked for fingerprints. I was hoping to get lucky. He bagged the bullet and said he would turn it over to the county crime lab. He thought we'd have an answer in a week or so. I hoped that would be soon enough. Maria seemed upset by what had happened so I tried to explain that I had some enemies from my previous professional life. I assured her that I knew full well how to care for her and myself as well. I decided that it was an opportune time for her to learn basic weapon handling. That afternoon I took her out back to let her shoot my Glock. I was surprised at how quickly she took to it. Within an hour she was hitting kill zones at thirty-five yards. Not bad for an ex-stockbroker I thought.

It was that evening that the nightmares began. I was starting to get back bits and pieces of that lost weekend. Men in white coats, needles, tape-recorded messages heard over and over again. The dream... the headaches... the memories were so unsettling that I couldn't get back to sleep. I went downstairs and made sure all the blinds were closed and doubled checked the locks on the doors and windows. I kept the lights out, sat down at my computer and logged on. I was anxious as I clicked the send and receive button. As expected, I was greeted with another message from the same anonymous sender that read,

I told you I was closer than you thought.
You cannot escape me.
The brotherhood of thieves awaits its revenge
The time of reckoning is near.

I suddenly felt pain in my temples and fell to my knees. I heard a buzzing sound from inside my head. I must have then blacked out as it was twenty minutes later when I next opened my eyes. The house was silent, only the gurgling of the stream outside was audible and the mournful sound of a faraway dove. I stumbled upstairs to the bedroom to retrieve several pieces of stolen military IT equipment then brought them back to my PC and attached them to the USB ports. I spent the next half hour hammering commands and codes. Then the final result appeared on the screen. My heart almost stopped. The messages I was receiving were coming from my laptop to my PC… it then immediately occurred to me… Maria. Now it all made perfect sense. Her seeking me out, a meeting not as chance as it first seemed, the quick romance, the conversation I overheard with the neighbors, her skill with the Glock. She was also the one who pushed for this specific house. How did she plan to get the money from the overseas account? Try and scare me into thinking someone from my past was close? Make me retrieve all the overseas cash before going on the lam? Then make her move? As I thought of her betrayal the rage swelled inside me. If I was right I didn't have much time … if not…

I went to the basement and got my garrote, then slowly climbed the stairs back to the loft where she lay, careful this time not to make the slightest sound that might disturb her sleep. I looked at her, overcome with sadness. The life I envisioned was now impossible. It had all been a charade, her love and affection merely tools to manipulate me. I kept the thoughts of her deceptions in my mind as I quickly wrapped the wire around her neck. Her eyes opened in shock as I quickly squeezed the life out of her. Tears fell on my hands as I removed the ligature.

It was close to seven a.m. when I finished burying her body in the woods about a hundred yards beyond the lake and in such a way that no wild animals would run across her corpse. I put on a pot of coffee and started to think. Was she the only one? Probably not. This smelled of a group effort. Who was she working with and how did she know about me? I had a few ideas. I sat on the couch thinking about any detail that might tip me off, reviewing the details of everyone I'd encountered since getting here and every conversation I had heard.

It was an hour later when I heard a car pull onto the gravel driveway. I looked through the front shade and saw Sheriff Masters exiting his vehicle. He walked slowly to the front door, which I opened before he could knock.

"Morning, Sheriff."

"Good morning, Mr. Hammersmith. I just wanted to give you some follow up. The lab identified three good fingerprints from the bullet. They said if the person is in their database, they should have an answer in a few days."

"That's great news. I appreciate you following up on this so quickly."

"Not a problem. Don't see much real police work out here. Mostly just our occasional DWI, domestic spats or illegally parked cars. Or maybe someone hunting out of season. Anyway, how's the missus doing? You got yourself a fine young lady there."

"Well, she had to leave town for a few days. She had some unfinished financial business in New York. I drove her to the airport early this morning."

"Well, give her my regards when you see her. Have you received any more threats?"

"No, things seemed to have quieted down. I'll let you know if there are any changes."

"Appreciate that. I'll call you as soon as I hear anything definite from the prints lab."

"Thank you," I said as the sheriff nodded his head and slowly walked back to his car. He stopped and looked at my car for a moment and then continued on. I went back to reading the newspaper to help me relax. It didn't help. I thought about all the work that needed to be done. I started packing my belongings and then cleaned and oiled my Sig .233 being overly cautious not to disturb the finely sighted optics. I knew I had work to do tonight.

John and Jessie were playing cards at their kitchen table. I was three hundred and twenty yards away and adjusted my scope for wind and distance. I took a steady prone position and concentrated. The gun popped twice in less than three seconds. Through the scope I watched each of their bodies drop lifelessly.

Several days passed. I had almost no sleep. My only nourishment came from a bottle of Jack Daniels. I had one panic attack after another. I slept with the lights on, waiting for someone to break in. I should be on the road, but couldn't pull myself together enough to leave. I couldn't get the visions of Maria's lifeless body out of my mind...

Then the headaches began. This was the worst it had ever been. I began to hear voices in my head... *you can't hide from who we're sending for you... we will be relentless...* I saw visions of the doctors... then a code from deep within... *the brotherhood of thieves... the brotherhood of thieves...* a buzzing sound in my skull... *you will self-destruct if you betray us...* I couldn't take it any longer. Death was the only thing I believed could bring me peace. I reached for my Glock and carefully chambered a round, my hands sweating and my eyes wild. I felt the cold steel in my mouth, as forces outside me seemed to slowly squeeze the trigger.

At that moment, the phone rang in the background breaking the excruciating tension. It rang three times then the answering machine picked up, "We're not home right now and you know the drill. Leave a number and a brief message and we'll get back to you at our earliest convenience." Beeep.

"Hello, Mr. Hammersmith, this is Sheriff Masters. Sorry to call at this hour, but I just received a call from the crime lab. I'm sorry it was no help. The only fingerprints they could identify were your own. Call me in the morning and I'll fill you in on all the details. Have a good night." A moment later, a single self- inflicted gunshot echoed off the finely crafted wooden beams causing a slumbering deer in the back yard to bolt upright and then take flight.

The phone rang in Lieutenant Colonel James Myer's plush office at Fort Dietrich. It was Dr. Frank Adams from Bethesda Naval Hospital.

"Hello, Jim. I wanted to review the autopsy findings and field investigation results in the triple homicide and suicide from Mystery Cove last week."

"Go ahead, Frank"

"Apparently this is related to an experimental nanotechnology program pioneered at ATC. We debriefed some of the psychiatrists and other medical personnel involved. It's hard to imagine but there was an implantable electronic microchip placed deep within the brain of some of the men who were part of the ATC. It was inserted with a stereotactic surgical needle by a neurosurgeon on the government's payroll. The chip was placed deep in the amygdala, the emotional center of the brain. It could be activated via satellite-based radio-signals and would trigger self-destructive behavior, suicide if you will. It was supposed to be used to take out any members who were captured and who might release highly classified information, or in this case, protection against the possibility of an agent gone bad."

"So it saves them a hell of a lot of time, effort, and guesswork in tracking down certain individuals. These guys are real gems. Makes the NSA look like the Girl Scouts," Myers said looking out his office window.

"Sure does. If an agent's been killed, the satellite activation will obviously do nothing. If they're still alive, well..."

"Then it triggers an auto self-destruct. Problem is there was a significant screw up here. Three innocent people down in collateral damage. Did you relay that to the white coats at the human guinea pig lab?" Myers asked as he started to pace around his office.

"Well, not exactly Jim... It's a bit more complicated than that," Adams reluctantly responded.

"What the hell do you mean?"

"Apparently the interrogation of Aaron Hansbeke was just completed. He was the Belgian member of the ATC group from Afghanistan. He survived a gunshot wound to the neck and was initially treated at an outpost Pakistani field hospital. Apparently he made some unsavory friends during his overseas assignment. He was presumed dead by coalition forces and he wanted everyone to continue thinking that. He made his way back to the states and started tracking down Roger Hammersmith, formerly one Agent

Roger Halstead. It took a while but he eventually found him in New York."

"If he wanted revenge why didn't he just put a bullet in Halstead and call it a day?"

"There were 2.5 million reasons why not: money taken from an Afghani heroin ring. He needed close access to get his hands on the money hidden in Halstead's AKA Hammersmith's overseas account. That's when he enlisted the aid of his sister, Maria and two cousins Jessie and John, both of whom had served time for drug trafficking. They tried to panic him, hoping he'd pull all the money back from overseas and get ready to run. Once they gained access to the money, Roger would undoubtedly have been killed. Apparently Roger caught wind of the plan and took matters into his own hands. He probably acted on less evidence than he might otherwise have. Since he was AWOL, the microchip implant was coincidentally activated via satellite around the same time. This induced a state of paranoia as well as activating the self-destruct command. Poor guy didn't have a chance. He got it from all sides. Real bad luck."

"And what's going on with this chip program?" Myers asked as he lit a cigar.

"I'm sure the military research folks will count this as a success. One dead rogue agent. Better shake your head and see if you hear anything rattling," laughed Adams.

Colonel Myers hung up and walked over to his bathroom mirror. He put down his handmade Monte Cristo cigar and began carefully examining the skin under his crew cut hair. There was a weekend or two he couldn't account for very well.

GRAY SKY OF SUMMER

As I remember him, my best friend of thirty years ago, Jimmy Bauer was thin as a reed with bright red hair and a face full of freckles. His voice was a bit high-pitched for a boy of fourteen. I can still hear him yelling from the driveway outside my bedroom…

"Frankie… Frankie! Get ya nose outta ya book and come outside. It's an awesome day out here and I brought my football. C'mon, let's play some catch." And with that I would pop-up from my bed, toss my latest comic book onto the dresser and pull on my blue mesh sports jersey. It had the number seventy-nine, carefully placed with silver duct tape, in honor of hero Harvey Martin. Speeding through the kitchen I'd give a quick nod to my mother, lunge down the front stairs two at a time (sometimes three), slide out the door, and immediately run a long pattern across the front yard. Jimmy would cock his long scrawny arm and lob me the ball as I imagined scoring the winning touchdown. We'd tackle each other and sometimes re-live our favorite professional wresting moves. Inevitably mom would put a temporary halt on all our youthful exuberance. At that point we'd head out for a long walk and talk about whatever was our hot topic of the day. Before setting out my mother would always have a word or two with us.

"Frankie and Jimmy, come here. Be careful, and no playing near Johnson's Stream," she would admonish. "There are too many slippery rocks and we don't need another broken bone around here. And Frankie I want you home no later than 5:30 for dinner… 5:30 the latest!"

I would yell "OK, mom," as Jimmy and I sped off into the lush green fields overgrown with cattails and wild lilac bushes. We jumped over fallen trees like Olympic hurdlers, and dodged angry yellow jackets that we stirred into flight as we ran through yellow and orange fields of marigolds. Before long we would be thick into the ten thousand acres of surrounding forest known to us simply as "The Pines." It was there that we would expend our seemingly endless stores of free-spirited energy. Like pups let out of a pet store cages, we would run, jump and yell at the top of our lungs, simply because we could. Half a mile into the Pines there was a tall elm tree with a large green canopy. It had a long thick branch jutting out almost eight feet off the ground with a twisted gnarl of smaller branches at the end that curved upward. It looked like a giant one-armed mother solemnly beckoning her young to come home. Jimmy, being the adventurous daredevil of our pair, would climb the tree and shimmy out onto the branch like a lizard scaling a stone wall. With help and several hard tugs from Jimmy on my outstretched arm, I would be pulled into the tree as well. The branch then became a majestic medieval horse upon which we, the two knights, rode to the castle to receive all the accolades that were justly deserved by such brave and fearsome warriors.

Our summers, always beautiful in Upstate New York, allowed our imaginations to flourish. There was always a toad to chase or salamander to catch. Sneaking down to Johnson's Stream, there were stones to skip and crayfish to find under rocks. My basement held a dozen or more tadpoles in a bucket that I watched incredulously change into small frogs. Night time meant a double scoop of maple walnut ice cream at the Frosty Treat and if we were good, we'd take weekly turns sleeping at each other's houses.

Neither of us could ever imagine growing up or not being best friends.

It was early August, just after dinner, when Jimmy stopped over. I heard my mom answer the front door.

"Hi, Jimmy. Come in… Frankie's just finished his dinner. He's still in the kitchen. Have you eaten yet?"

"Yes, thank you anyway," Jimmy said while he turned the corner from the living room and came into the kitchen. He tossed me a softball. "Hey there, how about a trip to The Pines?" He said with a touch of mischief in his voice.

"Don't you think it's a little late? It's almost six-thirty."

"Just for a bit. We won't stay long. I'll tell you more when we get outside. I've got an idea" Reluctantly, I followed him onto the front lawn.

"So, what's up Jimmy?" I asked, only half wanting to know. Whenever he was secretive, it usually meant I'd eventually be seeing the inside of my room for the evening, if not my father's belt.

"I was talking to Donny Sullivan this afternoon. He says a few miles into the Pines, down past old man Huntley's farm, there's an old abandoned house. It's pretty far off the main road and covered by a bunch of old trees and stuff."

"That's gotta be five miles from here, past the town line into Brandt. We'll never be back before nine."

"Oh yes we will. We gotta leave right now. No dilly-dallying. We can ride our bikes up to the farm and walk the last few miles."

"I don't like this. I see trouble," I said trying to sound convincing.

140

"Come on, don't be a chicken. Maybe there's some cool stuff in the house. Maybe even some forgotten money hidden away. Lots of people don't like banks. Maybe the owner died and nobody got the money. Donny didn't go in. He said it was creepy lookin'." That was enough for me. Creepy abandoned houses, even during the day, were not an enticement. At night there was no way.

"No thanks," I said curtly.

"OK, I'll go alone then." That always got me. I wasn't sure if it was a subconscious concern over Jimmy's safety or a nagging fear I would miss out on something exciting, but eventually, I gave in.

"All right, I'll go with you, but we have to be back by nine!"

"Not a problem," he said as we jumped on our bikes and peddled like bandits to old man Huntley's farm. We hid our bikes in his cornfield and then headed into the Pines on foot.

After almost half an hour of negotiating ravines, pulling burrs off my pants and walking through mud, I heard Jimmy exclaim, "There it is! Come and look!" I quickly climbed to the top of a large knoll and fifty yards into a clearing I saw it. A gray cedar farmhouse, most of the windows broken and the dilapidated front door hanging half off its badly rusted hinges. Donny had it right, this place looked creepy. We walked up alongside of it. The front stairs were gone and the railings were noticeably warped. The slate roof had several basketball-sized holes and spider webs covered large swaths of the front porch. An old rocking chair sat discarded in one corner.

"Come on, let's go in and take a look around," Jimmy said, the excitement mixed with fear mounting in his voice.

"It's getting late, Jimmy, let's come back another time."

"Are you crazy? After what it took to get here, we're going in. We gotta." Jimmy jumped onto the front porch and then helped hoist me up. The boards creaked with each step and I was sure it was only a matter of time before they collapsed and we would be stranded in some subterranean hole, an unexpected meal for the dozens of mice I'd seen scurrying around. With great effort we managed to pull open the dilapidated front door enough to squeeze inside. After knocking several rather large spiders from my shirt, I stood and admired the large two-story foyer. When in repair, it must have been a magnificent place. The dining room had a few vestiges of high end tables and chairs and a large rustic picture hung from one of the side walls, a few broken glasses and pieces of rusted silverware lay on a small end table. The room connected to a large kitchen with an opening leading to the basement. Jimmy was excited about a few coins he found in the living room. He was sure this was a sign of the large stash of cash we would inevitably uncover. I was starting to sneeze from the dust and ready to leave. The sun was setting, and I was feeling uneasy. Although it looked like nobody had lived here for many years I felt a strange uneasiness, as if someone else was with us. I couldn't shake the thought.

"Let's check out the basement, that's where they would keep the valuable stuff," Jimmy said sounding much too enthusiastic.

"We don't have a flashlight and it's getting pretty dark. We won't be able to see anything." I tried to logically dissuade him from going down there.

"Naw, it's still light enough if we hurry. So come on slowpoke." We started a slow descent, checking each step for its sturdiness before moving down. After a few minutes, we made it to the bottom. The basement was large and divided into three rooms. The largest was a food storage room, presumably for vegetables and canned goods. We walked over to it and tried to open the door, which was heavy as well as warped, causing it to stick to the wall. Just as we moved it a few inches, we heard what sounded like the door upstairs open.

"Shhh, quiet. Don't move Jimmy." We both listened from a dark corner in the basement; our eyes wide open, dust and sweat covering our faces. For a moment, there was no sound. Maybe it was just the wind or some of the mice scampering about. Then we heard footsteps on the floor above. There was a distinct creaking of the boards... moving slowly but deliberately closer to the cellar door.

"Let's hide," Jimmy said, his breath coming quicker. "There's no use, the only way out is up those stairs," I retorted.

"Maybe it's Donny Sullivan," Jimmy said hopefully but without much conviction in his voice.

A moment later the doorway leading to the basement filled with a form... one that was definitely not Donny Sullivan's. There was just enough light form the open doorway to illuminate the strange visage. It was that of a very old man, thin and hunched over. A wooden walking stick helped to steady him. He was nearly bald, with long matted gray hair draping the back of his neck. His nose was large and curved with several skin imperfections scaring his face.

"Hello?" he said in a raspy voice followed by a short high-pitched laugh. "I wasn't expecting visitors but I'm always glad to have some. If there is anyone down there, why don't you come up the stairs?" We didn't move an inch, trying not to even take a breath. "I can lock the door for the night, guess it wouldn't hurt if nobody's down there." The thought of spending the night in this basement and the punishment we'd get from our parents, if the old man didn't make stew of us, was too much. We waited a moment and looked into each other's eyes. Eventually Jimmy and I moved slowly towards the stairs, too scared to speak. "Come on up, there's no need to be afraid. I won't bite you... don't even have any teeth... heh... heh." We slowly slinked up the first steps... we were almost at the top when Jimmy blurted out, "We're sorry mister... we didn't know anybody lived here... we thought..."

"Hold on boys... hold on... it's all right," the old man interrupted. "I understand your confusion. Haven't really kept the place up very well now, have I?" He pulled two chairs from an old wooden desk and asked us to sit down. "What brings you to my house? And what were you looking for downstairs?" I glanced at Jimmy, my throat dry and tight. I wondered if we should just make a run for it. The old man didn't look like he could move too fast. Then Jimmy spoke, his voice even higher pitched than usual.

"We thought we might find a hidden treasure or some real old antiques we could sell. Believe me mister, we thought this place was abandoned," he said, almost pleading to be believed.

"Well, now that you're here, I think I might enjoy the company… and perhaps I can help you find that treasure you were looking for… or maybe something even greater than a treasure," he said as he smiled a toothless smile, his purple gums glistening with yellow mucus. He took a labored breath and gazed vacantly out the broken front window. His bluish lower lip quivered as he added, "You need to be brave to find it. So I ask, are you interested boys?"

Jimmy answered, "Sure we are, aren't we Frankie?"

I offered a meek "Yes," thinking about the trouble I'd be in if I didn't get home pretty soon.

"Well there's a very old cemetery about a mile from here. It's a Civil War burial ground. I've been told that one of the graves contains something special. I can't be sure, but I have heard that from an extremely trustworthy source. Not many would be brave enough to venture there. I sense you boys might have the courage to do so. Am I right?"

At this point I was willing to say anything to get out of there. I was starting to get really panicked. "Okay, sir, just tell us where to go, we'll dig it up." Over the next ten minutes the old man gave us directions and specified the tools we would need to complete the ghoulish task. Digging up an old grave, it seemed perfectly insane. I decided to play along so I could get out of there. In reality, I had no intention of going anywhere near a cemetery. I didn't care what mystical thing we'd find or how much money was buried there. Eventually the old man let us go, I was shocked we didn't end up on his dinner plate and we never moved so quick to get home.

I was at my front door a half an hour past my curfew. I was fortunate my parents had some friends over to play bridge and they had lost track of time. I slipped into the house, said a quick hello and quietly retreated to my bedroom. That night I didn't sleep well. I saw the old toothless man's grin, his greasy hair and his tattered clothes. His raspy voiced echoed in my head. When I awoke, I wondered if the whole thing had been a dream, a very bad one. I secretly hoped it had been. I was still sleeping restlessly when Jimmy jumped into my bed, pulling down the covers and shaking me awake.

"Come on Rip Van Winkle, it's almost ten o'clock," he shouted. "Your mom said to wake you up. Breakfast is over and you're gonna sleep right past lunch." I looked at him with disdain. I couldn't care less about breakfast or lunch. I wanted to sleep… and not to see the old man's face. With Jimmy's incessant prompting, I grudgingly got dressed and half-heartedly had some toast. Afterwards, we played in some of the hay bales piled up in the yard. For most of the afternoon neither of us mentioned the old house, the old man or what he had told us. Then for no apparent reason, Jimmy looked at me and said, "Where does your dad keep his shovels? We'll need a couple of spades and a crowbar."

"For what?" I asked with some trepidation.

"To find out what's hidden in that grave, stupid." After a long heated discussion, and for reasons I don't clearly remember, I finally consented to go. We rummaged through my father's tool shed, looking for a shovel light enough to carry on a bike. A small spade was located behind an old propane gas tank and a square shovel, with a beat up wooden handle was found hanging from a nail on the wall. We wrapped the spade and shovel in an old bed sheet. My family was hosting a dinner party celebrating my Uncle Mark's 50th birthday. That kept us busy until early evening. I wanted to get going quickly, the sun was starting to sink. Digging in a graveyard was unpleasant enough, doing it at night only added to my sense of dread about this whole affair.

With all the relatives milling around and the festivities keeping my parents occupied, it was easy to slip away unnoticed. We gathered up our digging implements, secured them to our bikes and road down to Huntley's farm. We rested and took a moment to review the old man's directions. We placed our bikes behind some lilac bushes and headed out into the woods. We eventually passed within about one hundred fifty yards of the house, but the old man was not on the porch. There were no lights lit. The sun was beginning to disappear and was being replaced by a waning gibbous moon. We still had nearly a mile to travel. My heart was already racing. Finally, after passing a decaying cornfield, we saw it. A small and unkempt cemetery stood before us. I counted fifteen, maybe twenty headstones at most. Many were severely cracked and worn. A few had fallen over, lying helplessly face down. The inscriptions, when they could be read were mostly middle to late eighteen hundreds. The oldest stone was from eighteen-twelve. I walked around wondering who these people were, some of whom were only infants or children at the time of death. I thought about their lives, how they might have run and laughed in the very fields upon which we traversed to arrive at this lonely forsaken boneyard. They played, no different than we did. They dreamed our thoughts and hoped our hopes. They also thought their days would never end.

"Come on Frankie, stop your day-dreaming. Let's get digging!" While my mind had wandered, Jimmy had located the spot. The headstone, gray and white, was plain looking. It bore no inscription. The dirt around it was soft from the rains of the previous two days. Our shovel and spade sank deep into the earth, mounds of dirt quickly grew around us. We worked feverishly, talking little over the next hour. The hole was four feet deep, but still nothing. We rested for a few moments then started in again. The sun was now completely gone, the moon provided our only natural light. We lit a small kerosene lantern and set it next to the hole. Half an hour later, nearly exhausted and gulping air, I heard Jimmy's shovel hit something solid.

"We found it… we…" he said, between labored breaths. In a few moments we had the top cleared and brought down the lantern. It was the top of an octagon shaped coffin, pine wood and musty smelling. It was sealed by a padlock and a small rusted chain. We stared at each other for a moment in the cramped space. With the ground being so wet, I was momentarily afraid we wouldn't be able to climb out of the hole … if we had to. Jimmy took his spade and began frantically hitting the lock. "Come on," he said. "Let's get this thing opened." He used the spade a dozen times before one of the chain links finally broke. We bent the link and slid it around the coffin's steel latch. I grabbed the lantern, bringing it close to the broken lock. Jimmy took it from my hand and grasped for the edge of the coffin's lid. I instinctively turned away. I heard the lid creak and piece of wood break, then a few seconds of silence. Suddenly, Jimmy screamed. He bellowed out a visceral, guttural scream. He dropped the coffin lid and lantern and using my thigh as a ledge, he scampered up the hole's muddy wall and ran off. I heard his screams slowly fade. I felt my heart pounding and my hands became wet. I turned to try and climb out, and then stopped. I had come this far… I had to see for myself. Against all reason, I held up the lantern. I reached down and lifted the lid. It was dark at first, and then I pushed the lid completely open. I bent over, eyes half closed and looked. I was shocked… completely astonished at what I saw inside the coffin. For a moment I was frozen in disbelief. Then I began to cry, at first a whimper… then inconsolably. The lantern slipped from my hand and fell into the thick mud. I trembled as tears fell from my face… onto my body's reflection in the full-length mirror that lay at the bottom of the octagon box.

Strange as it sounds, Jimmy and I never spoke of that day and what transpired in the old cemetery. The remainder of the summer passed uneventfully and soon our next year of school began. After that summer, I remember maple walnut ice cream cones never quite tasting as rich and The Pines losing some of their mystique and excitement. I never again ran through the fields of marigolds with the unbridled joy and reckless abandon that are the consorts only of the young and naïve in spirit. Jimmy and I slowly grew apart over the next few years. A friendship I thought would last forever slowly withered and one day Jimmy's family relocated to Pennsylvania. We'd talk on the phone now and again and promised to meet up sometime but that never happened. It's been more than twenty years since we've last spoken. There are times when I really miss him. I also miss our time in The Pines when we were able to run fast and far enough to outpace the harsh realities of life at least for that moment, a moment that we mistakenly thought would last forever.

JUST DESSERT

I was nervous, fidgeting, my eyes darting as I anticipated her arrival. Other patrons sat comfortably around me, perusing their maroon leather-bound menus while gazing at the ornate decorum of the regionally acclaimed White House Inn. My eyes occasionally fixed on the large leaded glass door flanked by Grecian columns that showcased the two-story foyer adjacent to the main dining area. My right hand fumbled with my tie while my left slowly rubbed the lacy white linen tablecloth. The sound of silverware and china clinking in the background merged imperceptibly with the hum of a dozen different conversations. Those around me seemed lost in their individual worlds. Without realizing it I caught myself eavesdropping on a conversation at a nearby table. There seemed to be a rather heated debate over the most appropriate location of the next summer cottage rental. I was certain I would soon be the victim of such auditory voyeurism once my dinner guest arrived. My eyes methodically scanned the room then settled on my antique silver pocket watch. It was six thirty-four. She was late again, but why should I be surprised? This was surely a dinner she would like to avoid. I felt palpitations within my chest as I looked out the window, nervously searching the parking lot for her car. Part of me wanted her to not show up but another part knew she must. A portly waiter, looking tired and ill- suited for the formal black tuxedo he wore, brought me a glass of Merlot before lumbering back into the kitchen. I took a large swallow hoping for some small sedative effect. However, the anxiety remained. Waiting did at least give me a chance to reflect on how we got to this point.

It's hard to recall exactly why I hated her so much, after all, she was my brother's wife. Time had obscured the original events, which so strongly stirred my emotions. It was no one thing, as I remember, but slowly I came to see her as a dark and foreboding presence. Her manner was not unlike a callous physician bringing bad news to an ailing patient. I knew she was a phony from the start. She was someone who had only her own best interests in mind. She could never be bested. As my grandmother once said, "If your shoes are green, hers had to be greener." She continually demanded respect but failed to give any in return. She dressed to perfection with never a hair out of place or a nail not recently manicured at the trendiest salon. Her clothes were all top shelf designer and she was proud to have paid full price. The cell phone always rang perfectly timed to interrupt a family event, confirming her importance to anyone around. She telegraphed the subtle but distinct feeling she was inconvenienced to be in our presence or burdened to attend an event where she wasn't the center of attention. I won't forget the snide remarks about my profession, that of a pharmacy technician, which she continuously noted required little schooling beyond the high school years. She made it clear I was no intellectual match for her Ivy League MBA and there was certainly no comparison in our relative monetary compensations.

If that's all there was, it could have been tolerated. Many, if not most, families have members that merely endure each other. That being the case perfunctory greetings and hollow well wishes at the requisite holiday get-togethers would suffice. Lives are lived separately and without regret. There is never a need for anything more. With her, however, it was different. Her personality was like an acid that ate at the very fabric of my soul. The mix of her pomposity and aloofness as well as an incessant need to diminish even the smallest joy in others caused a silent but ever growing rage to burn within me. Things had degenerated to the point where even a casual acknowledgement of each other's presence became impossible. When she strode into a room displaying her pearls and diamonds on a body she owed mostly to a very competent and very expensive plastic surgeon, I would avert my eyes and place my attention on some mundane task. The tension between us was thick as an early spring fog. A seemingly innocent comment could provoke a sharp exchange of words.

In the beginning family members encouraged us to reconcile. I was not adverse to this, but she would have nothing to do with it. This became especially true after a harsh encounter at a Thanksgiving Day meal almost ten years ago. Accusations flew and venom filled the air leading me to make an abrupt departure even before the main course was served. Six months had passed before we spoke another word to each other.

I spent many sleepless nights consumed by my growing hatred for this woman. I replayed each and every slight she made me suffer. Every free thought I had seemed to find its way to her. I would often construct a clever mental diatribe directed at her in order to sooth my nerves. Many nights my dreams were haunted by her presence causing me to awake distressed, my heart pounding and my trembling hands wet with sweat. Late one evening an idea came upon me that allowed some reclamation of my previously content character. I resolved it to myself that I would make every concession and any sacrifice to see her in a coffin. By that understand, I meant no direct harm to her, as I have said I am a gentle person by nature. My generous personality would be affirmed by anyone that knew me. I meant that I would do whatever necessary, to live a long and rewarding life. My all-consuming wish was to simply outlive her, then take great satisfaction in attending her funeral. This might sound callous, but anyone who was a recipient of a stare from her cold lifeless eyes would consider this desire to be quite tame. If I were to live only one day beyond her years I would have considered my time spent on this enterprise an unmitigated success.

To this end I strove with relentless enthusiasm. I threw away my cigarettes and avoided any place where smoke fouled the air. I purchased a membership to a gym, making use of all the current fitness technologies. I began isometric and isotonic muscle training and even started training for a 10K marathon. I used the Stairmaster and sweated on the elliptical, did dozens of sit-ups daily, and ran regularly on a treadmill. I drank whey protein shakes, fruit and kale smoothies and took vitamin and herbal supplements. I walked outside a brisk three miles every day and even availed myself to the tutelage of an Indian master who taught me the subtle techniques of Transcendental Meditation as part of a comprehensive stress reduction program. Sometimes in a deep relaxing trance, a vision of her lying in a casket with her fake smile molded in place by a skilled undertaker, would bring me close to a state of nirvanic rapture. I also took to disdaining meat. I lived on an abundant diet of fruits, vegetables, and legumes. With each steak or fried food that I willfully passed up, the vision of myself offering disingenuous condolences to her distraught family brought me to a profound state of bliss. Those euphoric thoughts made the sacrifice of forsaking even the most luscious of culinary delights seem insignificant. I gladly passed up muffuletta and steak au poivre, as well as penuche, pralines and prawns. No more blanquette de veau or andouillette. My health exams were stellar. My doctor was amazed at the progress I made and attributed it to my desire to see my young daughters married and to enjoy my grandchildren. My motive however was much more disturbing. Many of my coworkers asked for my secret of success, to which I would simply reply, "clean living", or I would smile at them with a mischievous grin, and tell them they would have to wait and read my new diet book. I assured them it wouldn't be long before I was a regular on Dr. Oz.

Although I saw my dear sister-in-law at regular family gatherings, she made no mention at my physical transformation. I heard her whisper to one of our cousins that I was probably taking steroids and it would eventually catch up with me. Steroids, ephedrine, growth hormone, creatine and any of a number of artificial enhancing agents were strictly off limits. They were certainly available and easily procured but they did not suit my purposes. It was not my design to have only the appearance of well-being but to actually be well. I subscribed to longevity magazines and even fasted one day a week. My mood and outlook on life improved dramatically. My job performance and efficiency at work led to several promotions with corresponding salary improvements. I was now the supervisor of distribution for the Englewood Pharmacy chain. I oversaw the delivery of various drugs and medical devices to twenty-five pharmacies as well as two hospitals and one research laboratory. I had more energy than I'd had in years. I bicycled, hiked, and spent occasional fall weekends camping in the mountains. My mind became fertile ground for new ideas. I spent hours reading pharmacology journals and even considered returning to school for a master's degree. I absorbed esoteric information that I stored with great satisfaction. My memory was the best it had ever been. I collected a plethora of facts that I could recall on demand. At office parties I would impress colleagues with trivia such as the chemical structure of cholesterol or DNA or the names and years in office of each respective U.S. president. I memorized each state's capital city, state flower, and bird. I loved learning science trivia. I knew that due to quirk of olfactory genetics only one in five people can detect the burnt almond smell of cyanide. A fact that helped several lucky pathologists crack an unsolved death. I even fascinated listeners with the fact that due to car accidents, white-tailed deer kill more people in the United States annually than serial killers. I stored hundreds of these seemingly meaningless facts. It became a game to see how much I could remember. Life was good and I was very happy.

Things suddenly changed on a late Friday afternoon when I got a call from my doctor's office. One of my blood tests had come back abnormal and they were a little concerned. It had been detected during my routine physical exam. I wasn't sure what it meant, or how serious it was. My doctor wanted to see me the following Monday. He told me many things might cause this type of result, most of which were harmless. Despite his reassurance, I fretted incessantly over the weekend with persistent worry and speculation. When I finally saw Dr. Reynolds he said my amylase level was elevated. He again told me that it might be nothing, but he wanted to order a CAT scan of my abdomen to be certain. He would schedule it as soon as possible.

The result was not good. It showed an enlargement of my pancreas. It was determined by Dr. Reynolds to be either some sort of localized infection or a tumor. Later that week a radiologist did what is called a CT guided needle biopsy and a pathologist diagnosed me with pancreatic cancer. I was completely shocked by this news. I had no symptoms and felt that I was in the best physical shape I had been in years. I was informed that with this type of malignancy, there is really no effective therapy. Dr. Reynolds anticipated that I had less than a year to live. In a split moment my life, once full of promise, took on the bleakest outlook. My mind was clouded with a bone deep depression that I was sure would never clear.

When I left the office I was in a daze. I screamed at God and hated every person I saw. How could they go about shopping, eating ice cream or walking their dogs when I was just told I had only months to live? This wasn't supposed to happen. I was supposed to live to ninety! I was not even fifty years old. Then the most terrifying and unsettling thought welled up within me. Her. She would be at my funeral, strutting around with transparent grief. I envisioned her pretending to console my brother, my wife and my kids. All the while she would secretly be laughing at my grievous misfortune. In reality, she would have no sympathy for my wife or daughters. She would be gloating under her long black silk dress and stylish high heels. Damn it, she will have bested me again. I could visualize her smug grin as she cast disparaging glances at my lifeless body. This thought slowly ate at me like maggots devouring

rotting meat. It was perhaps the one thing worse than knowing
death's shadow was now cast over me. It was a few weeks later I
first heard the murmurings of a proposed meeting; a plan for us to
set things straight.

My brother was the one pushing for the reconciliation
between her and I. He bullied, cajoled, and even tried to bribe me to
make amends with his wife. In reality there isn't very much you
can offer a man with a short time to live. Even someone on death
row holds out a hope of reprieve, a governor's midnight pardon, but
for those like myself, no such hope exists. There's only the three
a.m. existential loneliness know only to those terminally ill. At
some point you realize that time has become your enemy. Each
passing moment pulls you closer to the abyss. I resisted any
mending of the proverbial fences at first, wanting to simply have her
banned from attending my wake and funeral. Finally, after several
weeks of my brother's unremitting pressure, I gave in. He applied
the same techniques to his wife who eventually agreed to having
dinner with me in order to keep peace in her home, hence our date
for this evening.

Finally, I saw her new red Mercedes swing into the parking
lot and pull into a spot on the far side of the building, a full thirty
minutes late. "Not bad," I observed aloud to myself. At least she
showed up. I tensed as she strolled across the asphalt lot with a sour
look on her face. She passed through the main door and spoke
abruptly to the maitre de. She spotted me and walked briskly over
to the table and then took the chair across from me. It had a high,
elegantly carved cherry backrest making her look like a queen on a
throne.

"Hello, Jonathan."

"Hello, Maxine."

"Listen, Jonathan, let's just forget about this bullshit, huh? I'm here because your brother has been making my life miserable. He wants us to make amends before you're gone. Personally I don't really care. Dying or not, you're a sniveling little wretch of a man. Let's just pretend that things are better and end this little charade. It's the least you can do for your brother."

"Well Maxine, I'm glad you're not here under false pretenses."

Just then, our waiter arrived. He took our meal orders. Maxine was predictable if nothing else. She ordered the exact same entrée and dessert every time she ate at a five star restaurant. She claimed only the best chefs were qualified to prepare this type of food correctly. Unknown to most, she pontificated, desserts were even more dependent on a skilled culinary expert than the main dish. Her condescending attitude was at least one constant in this otherwise unpredictable world. I ordered gingered plum-glazed halibut, now that dietary excesses were not really of much concern.

"No I'm not going to erase ten years of despising you. I'm not a hypocrite. In fact, truth be told, I'm looking forward to your funeral. It will be the only time I won't mind being in the same room as you."

I sat flabbergasted. To show such disdain for a man with such a short time to live was even below the level of depravity I expected of her. In truth I had anticipated this encounter might go one of two very different ways. I was mentally prepared for either.

"Listen Maxine—"

"No, you listen. You tell your brother we patched things up and that we can at least tolerate each other. If not, I promise you I'll make life miserable for those two girls of yours. I have the connections to do that. Your widowed wife, who never worked a day in her life, won't be worth much once you're gone. With her limited finances she certainly won't be of much use to them. I can make sure your brother doesn't give them one red cent."

"Why you no good..." I was at a complete loss for words. My face was flushed crimson and I stood up and threw my napkin on the table. "I've had enough."

"That's fine with me, but remember what I said about the girls."

I stormed off briefly stopping by the kitchen. I wanted to give a courtesy explanation to the chef, whom I knew from several prior social contacts. Our daughters also attended the same high school and were friends. After a moment he noticed me standing among several of his junior chefs. I then had a short chat with him and briefly explained the situation. He was very understanding. I then took my leave through the service entrance and slipped into my car. As I looked back into the restaurant I saw Maxine still at the table. What had just transpired had so little impact on her that she evidently planned to stay and have dinner alone. I saw her speaking sharply to the waiter, no doubt making complaints about the quality of the wine or the poor service, or any of a myriad of other trivial complaints. I secretly watched the scene for the next ten minutes then finally drove off into a dark moonless night.

"And you're sure you'd like to cancel your veal marsala, madam?" asked the waiter apparently frustrated with the turn of events at his first table of the evening.

"Yes, am I not speaking English? Just dessert tonight."

"Yes madam, just dessert for you. And will your friend be returning?"

"He is not my friend and no he will not be returning," she laughed smugly to herself. No, soon, he would never be returning anywhere. She was quite pleased at how events had turned so pleasantly in her favor.

Maxine slowly savored the chocolate dipped almond anise biscotti. An unusual dessert she ordered without fail when dining out at better restaurants. I later heard she left a paltry tip as well as a sharp critique for the chef. She complained he was obviously very inexperienced in preparing almonds for her dessert. Those which crossed her palate were clearly overcooked, almost burnt according to her exquisite sense of taste.

The Medical Examiner's preliminary ruling on the cause of Maxine's death was undetermined. This wasn't surprising as toxicology results often take weeks to come back. I sat next to my brother and tried to console him. In my heart I knew that in the long run he would be better off without her. I gazed at the casket thinking about how small and insignificant she now looked. It took great control to hide my satisfaction that I had achieved what I sought. It was a moment later when the funeral director tapped me on the shoulder. He told me that I had an urgent phone call and that I could take it in his office.

"Hello, Jonathan, this is Dr. Reynolds. Please accept my deepest sympathy for the loss of you sister-in-law. I thought you'd be at her viewing, and didn't think this news should wait. I don't know quite how to say this, but there was a mistake made in the pathology lab. It seems there was a mix up with your biopsy and... well... the bottom line is that you don't have cancer. The enlargement we saw on your CAT scan was caused by pancreatitis, which is just an inflammation of the pancreas... not a malignancy. This type of infection can be effectively treated with a few weeks of antibiotics. We'll also need to check you for gallstones which can also be a cause of pancreatitis but we can do that in a few weeks. I called in a script and the pharmacy will have it ready for you this afternoon. I'm very sorry about this... I'm still waiting to hear back from the pathologist on how a mistake like this could have happened. I'm so sorry... this type of mistake has never happened to a patient of mine."

"Well I'm... um... well... speechless. I mean this is a lot to handle... I feel like crying... but at the same time I feel like running around the block, dancing, screaming... it's just so... I don't know what."

"Well, Jonathan, take a moment to settle down. The good news is that you're in extremely good health and should have at least another forty years to celebrate. Why don't you set up an appointment to see me early next week and by then I should have more details about what caused this mess and we can reevaluate your infection. Again let me offer you my condolences on the loss of your sister-in-law."

"Thank you, Dr. Reynolds, I'll plan on seeing you next week."

As I looked out the window my heart raced and the phone slowly slid out of my hand and bounced off the desk. Outside I noticed a sheriff's car pulling into the parking lot. In the back seat I recognized my friend, the chef, from the White House Inn. He was looking uneasily at the front door of the funeral home. Apparently the toxicology results must have come back a little sooner than I expected.

UNLUCKY SHOT

James Cartright waited months for this opportunity. He pulled his pickup truck a hundred yards from Frank Lawson's house, careful to park near several large oak trees. Once the lights were off the vehicle would be nearly impossible to see. Technically, Frank was James' next door neighbor, although their houses were nearly half a mile apart. Cartright killed the truck's engine and headlights. His watch read nine-o'clock. The tool bag clanked as he pulled it from the glove compartment. He then walked across the cornfield towards Lawson's house. He reached around to the small of his back and felt the bulge of his .38 Smith and Wesson. He knew he would never use it, but the secure feeling it brought was welcome.

Lawson was at his weekly lodge meeting. Some order of the Moose or some other damn animal. Having been his neighbor for over ten years, Cartright knew of Lawson's distrust of banks. He kept his savings, over sixty thousand dollars he heard Lawson boast one night after too much beer, hidden under the basement's wooden floorboards. Cartright slipped on his mask and reached into his coat pocket. He smiled, noticing the raw steak was still cold. He had thought of everything.

With little effort Cartright opened the rear door and entered the kitchen. Just as he expected he heard a loud noise as Baxter barreled down the stairs and turned the corner to face him. The two hundred fifty pound English Mastiff was a formidable sight. Cartright talked calmly, stretching each syllable as if talking to a newborn. After a moment he tossed the pound of raw meat on the floor. Baxter wagged his tail and began devouring the steak, happily letting Cartright pass. "Ha, man's best friend... big dumb mutt…" Cartright laughed to himself. Betraying the house for a pound of flesh, he snickered as he crept down the basement stairs. Glad I have cats, he thought. At least *you knew* they never had your back.

The wooden planks covering the money were soon torn away and Cartright scooped the cash into a bag. He had been careful to wear shoes two sizes too big as well as latex gloves. The local police were not Einsteins, but why take any chances? He got to the top of the stairs and stopped suddenly. His heart pounded when a car turned into the driveway. He surreptitiously peered out the window and saw it was Frank. He was home forty-five minutes early. Cartright quickly hid behind a large cabinet near the entrance to the kitchen and waited. As soon as the door opened he lunged at Lawson pushing him hard against the wall. He hoped to scare the hell out of him and then run his ass off out of there and disappear into the woods.

"Who the hell are you?" he yelled as he pulled himself up. There was no answer as Cartright attempted to flee. Lawson grabbed his assailant and drove him hard into the floor. Cartright's head spun backwards and he felt the room spin. Lawson held him down and pulled off the mask.

"My God… Jim? How could you?" Lawson freed one hand and pulled open the bag spilling some of the stolen money onto the floor. "I'll have you arrested you no good bastard. You'll do five years and deserve every one of them!" The thought of prison caused him to panic. He could never do hard time. He fought hard and slipped out of Lawson's grasp. Without thinking, he grabbed his gun. Lawson froze not moving from the floor. From within the dark house there was a commotion and suddenly Baxter appeared, growling. grrr... grrr... his large white teeth showing under his snarling lips. Cartright was in no mood to be mauled and tried to flee. Secretly he hoped Lawson would cool down and could be eventually talked out of notifying the cops. Unfortunately for him, Lawson was not in a forgiving mood and saw red. He crashed into Cartright causing both to tumble down the basement steps. Once they hit the bottom, Cartright jumped quickly to his feet, pointed the gun, and fired a single shot. Lawson fell with a thud, dead on the spot. Lucky shot. In the darkness, the large Mastiff moved towards the stairs. Cartright then turned and fired a shot to scare off the massive canine. After the shot, the dog lumbered away quickly and then disappeared. Cartright's nerves were completely frayed as he quickly ascended the stairs and gathered the money. He took the opportunity to make his escape, slamming the door and running through the fields back to his truck.

Ten minutes later he collapsed exhausted on his bed. He slept very uneasy that night. He had no appetite and felt sick about what occurred. The whole day he went over and over what had happened. Did he leave any evidence? Did anyone hear the scuffle or the gunshots? Did anyone see his truck? He hoped the isolation of the house provided a firm "No" to each of his concerns.

It was just after dinner that the knock came on the door. He opened it seeing a police car parked in his driveway and a uniformed officer on his porch.

"Hello, Jim, Sheriff Brian Kempson here. I expect you heard Frank Lawson was killed last night during a robbery. May I come in and talk to you?"

"Of course, Sheriff, I'm terribly upset. I heard the bad news earlier on the radio, absolutely horrible. You'd think living out here in the sticks would give us some measure of security. Any suspects? I'm a little nervous being so close to a murder." Cartright's face was white and his palms were wet as he led the sheriff to a chair.

"I don't want to go into any details, but was wondering if you saw or heard anything unusual last night, most likely between nine and ten o'clock?"

"No, sheriff. I'm sorry, I didn't. I was in the shed tinkering with a tractor engine. I didn't hear or see anything out of the ordinary."

"Our records indicate you own a .38 handgun, is that correct?" Cartright felt his stomach drop. The acid secretions caused his stomach to ache. He had burned all the clothes he wore so there was no gunpowder residue to detect. The gloves had kept his hands unblemished. The gun was thoroughly cleaned and oiled this morning.

"Yes, I do Sheriff, but I guess a quarter of the men in town have one… is that how Frank was killed?"

"Yes, a single gunshot in the head. The medical examiner recovered the bullet, but it's useless from a ballistics standpoint. It was severely damaged by the impact with his skull. I don't want to worry you, but can I see your gun? We're checking on everyone in the area who owns one. I trust you'll cooperate without a warrant. It really is just a routine check. I know both of you were friends." Cartright let out a sigh of relief and went over to his American Security safe, unlocked the massive steel door and retrieved his handgun.

"Here you go, Sheriff, it's all yours," he said smiling. The sheriff looked at the gun carefully convinced it hadn't been fired recently.

"I guess I don't need to keep this. Your pistol permit is up to date, you've had no violations." Just then a repetitive high-pitched sound filled the room. Sheriff Kempson reached for his beeper. He pushed a button and observed the phone number. "Mind if I borrow your phone Jim? My cell is in the squad car."

"Be my guest Sheriff," he said pointing towards the kitchen.

"Holy Moses, you have got to be kidding me…why ain't that …" a moment later the sheriff hung up. "You're not going to believe this one," he said smiling.

"What's that Sheriff?" Cartright said looking puzzled.

"Well that was my deputy, Ed Carter. He was calling from the Oakfield Veterinary clinic. Turns out someone brought Lawson's dog there this morning. They found him limping out on the interstate. The vet takes an x-ray and finds a bullet lodged in his thigh. Now this dog is so big, the bullet got stuck in fat and muscle and according to the vet, it is in pristine condition. The boys in ballistics aren't going to believe this one. Should be easy to match it to the weapon that fired it. Just to clear you right off the bat, why don't I have ballistics check your gun this afternoon and I'll have it back to you tomorrow morning. That way you can get on with your business and put this unfortunate event behind you. You don't need me to fuss about getting a warrant do you?" he said as he placed the gun in a brown evidence bag. Cartright felt the shooting pains begin again in his stomach.

"No sheriff, a warrant isn't necessary. What would I have to hide?"

THE PARTY

So this is what it's like to be dying she thought. The journey provoked more fear than the destination. She rolled past stained aureolin yellow walls on a gurney much bigger than her contracted body. It made her look like a toddler asleep in a parent's bed. She attempted a perfunctory straightening of her disheveled gray hair, not that she believed anyone was really paying attention. Either way, it was no use. Her twisted fingers with unnatural bumps seemed glued to each other. Her arms would not obey her wishes, seeming to know she was no longer in command. She was not herself and hadn't been for quite some time. The chemotherapy made her wrinkled skin as parched as desert sand. Weight loss caused her loose skin to look like an oversized blanket thrown atop a pile of discarded bones. The attempt to fix her hair was really just instinct; a throwback to the days when she was a young beauty who captured the attention of every schoolboy. She was never conceited but always took care to present herself properly. Her mother Constance often reminded her that "first impressions are with the eyes and only later will the ears have their say." She was fortunate to possess a striking natural beauty that neither cosmetics nor expensive apparel could do much to improve. Her elegant looks did not begin to fade until long after the disease came.

The gurney bumped along the corridor, occasionally throwing her thin, sickly body into the air. She winced as she was pressed against the cold steel side rail whenever a turn was made too quickly. Her whole body hurt from the cancer, but she made no complaint. She was whisked up from the emergency department onto a dilapidated elevator. Several people boarded with her and eyed her as unobtrusively as possible. She felt uncomfortable, the unwanted center of attention. Her fellow passengers mumbled to themselves about the weather and small personal problems while she stared silently at the white grated ceiling. She was secretly jealous they would get to leave today. It was hot and she was having trouble breathing, her lungs heavy bags of concrete. She was glad to see the doors finally part on the seventh floor. The attendant, a young man looking barely twenty, turned the corner sharply and wheeled her past the nursing station and into the room. He pulled out the earplugs from his iPod and pushed a pedal that brought the stretcher to a sudden halt with a loud metallic clank. So this is where I'll die she thought.

"This is room 712B, Mrs. Antoni. Not the Waldorf Astoria, but not bad for a county hospital," he chuckled softly as he unfastened the gray cloth belt that held her as tightly as a lover reluctant to depart.

"At least there is a view of the park. I don't think I could have looked at the parking ramp all day," she said with labored breath. She glanced out the window and looked down towards the black asphalt road that snaked along the edge of the Veterans' Park. She watched as several school buses slowly drove past. The deep melodic hum of their engines soothed her in an unexpected way. Since it was a Saturday, she thought the children might be on their way to a sporting event or perhaps a field trip to see a play. She smiled, imagining the excited chatter echoing inside each bus as the children looked forward to the day. She secretly wished she could be ten again.

"You got that, Mrs. Antoni. Gotta be thankful for little blessings. You coulda gotten the other bed and only had the hallway to look at. Plus you'd have to listen to those nurses complaining all day about too much work… too many patients. Right now you don't have a roommate, so enjoy the quiet."

She strained to lift her head, "Oh, but I've never liked it quiet. I was always one to run and do… dinner with friends, perhaps a concert… most of them are gone now… or spending part of the summer at the lake house… beach vacations, and especially sailing on the lake. I love the water… was a pretty good sailor in my time. I wasn't always the withered old lady you're looking at," she said with a touch of pride as she took a series of labored breaths followed by a brief coughing spell.

"Old lady? Who said old lady?" he smiled feigning a surprised voice. Charlotte smiled at the kind gesture. She strained to help him slide herself onto the hard bed. The sheets felt chilled and crinkled loudly as her legs fell upon them like stumps from trees long dead. She grabbed at her wispy blue hospital gown and attempted to cover her half naked body, which was marked with heavy black "X's" that helped guide the radiation treatments.

"I'm sorry," she said in a hushed tone, her face crimson with embarrassment at the unwanted exposure. After all the indignities she had been through the past year she thought she would have gotten used to it… but she never did. In a strange way she thought of this illness as some spiritual failure on her part.

Sensing her discomfort the attendant spoke up, "Not a problem. These gowns are made for fashion models not real people. Happens every day… even to me when I had my appendix out. I think whoever designed these things should wear them around town for a week… I'm sure that would solve the problem." She smiled at that idea and felt a touch less self-conscious.

As she helped settle herself in the bed the stiff plastic covered pillow crunched as she fell back. She began puffing like a steam engine, almost completely out of breath. Laughing to herself, she remembered when she led the Sacred Heart track team to the county finals. People called her a gazelle. What would they think now? Her once lean, muscular legs looked more like desiccated tree branches than a graceful animal from the Serengeti.

"There you go. I hope you're comfortable. Doctor Connors should be in shortly to check in on you. He's on call and making rounds this weekend. Someone from TV and telephone should drop by soon."

In a trembling voice not much above a whisper she said, "Oh my dear boy, I don't need either. I'm eighty-five. Most of the people that would truly care to talk to me have already passed and everyone else would call only out of obligation… and as for TV, well, my eyes aren't very good. Now a radio, that's something that I would pay for. I remember listening to Benny Goodman or Artie Shaw on Saturday nights with my family. We huddled together around that big brown Philco and ate hot popcorn all night. My mother adored George Burns. My dad loved Arthur Godfrey and never missed the Danny Kaye Show." Her tight lips smiled gently at the memory.

"All right, let me see what I can do."

"Thank you. By the way, you never told me your name."

"I'm sorry. I'm José Tempora. I hate wearing those Hospital ID badges. I've gotten into trouble more than once for it… bad picture. Looks worse than a mug shot, not that I've ever had one."

"Well José, it was nice meeting you."

He nodded, "Same here," then maneuvered the stretcher out the door and quickly disappeared down the hallway. As she watched him walk confidently from the room she suddenly felt jealous, being no longer able to move about on her own. Such a simple thing she had taken for granted for so many years. She was restless. Her arms flailed and legs pushed but she failed to find a comfortable position. Somehow, after a long while, sleep eventually came. She dreamt of her tenth birthday party. It was a brilliant warm late May afternoon. The dogwoods and azaleas colored the yard like an impressionist painting. The crabapple and aristocratic pear trees were in full bloom forming a colorful canopy in the yard's narrow walkway. The bright sun cut through the red maple trees illuminating two deep red cardinals perched on one of their branches. The day started with her father taking her to breakfast at her favorite restaurant. She had stacked banana oatmeal pancakes with blueberry syrup and drank fresh squeezed orange juice. When she arrived home the house was decorated with streamers and balloons of every color. A warm wind occasionally gusted through the house causing the colorful papier-mâché streamers on the walls to flutter like the wings of a hummingbird searching for nectar. Several ornate presents wrapped with meticulous care and topped with brightly colored bows sat atop the kitchen table.

Later, many school friends and half a dozen cousins sang an out of tune but very enthusiastic rendition of "Happy Birthday" to her. This was her first birthday celebration at the new home on

Third Street. The children played all afternoon in the yard, running and hiding and laughing so hard they could hardly talk. Her grandparents were there and fussed over her. Grandma straightened her dress as she fidgeted, anxious to get back to play with the other children. Her mother unsuccessfully called her over and tried to fix her long black hair. For her gift, her parents bought her a beautiful white gold ring with her initials and birth date etched inside. She had seen it in the jewelry store months prior and couldn't believe it was now hers. She was so happy that day. She couldn't imagine the world a more wonderful and vibrant place. When she had a moment to herself she clasped her hands tightly and secretly wished and prayed this day would never end.

When her grandfather saw her he scooped her in the air, turned her upside down and spun her around. She laughed so hard she could hardly breathe. After regaining her balance she snuck her hand into his jacket pocket and pulled out a piece of candy. It was a game he taught her when she was just a toddler. Whenever he came over, he would say in a long drawn out voice, "I've gotten something special, a sweet treat for you, but you have to find it." He would hide a candy bar, or small toy in one of his pockets and she would probe each one until she found the treat. Then she quickly ran off, lest one of her older siblings would clamor for her to share the treasure. Over the years she had become so adept at finding the hidden treats that she often had it in hand before her grandfather knew it was gone, no matter how skillfully hidden.

The squeak of the hospital door opening awakened her. "Hello, excuse me... Mrs. Antoni. I'm Dr. Connors." Her eyes peered from above the standard issue brown hospital blanket. She was smiling, not fully awake, the dream so real she believed for a moment she was a little girl again. She was a bit resentful that the doctor had interrupted such a pleasant moment; she had so few in the last months.

"Hello, doctor. I suppose you're here to push some medicine on me. You know I've never been one to beat around the bush so let me say straight off, I've no desire to do anymore. No more therapies for me." She coughed spasmodically for a moment before catching her breath and it took a moment for her to settle herself.

"Well, you seem quite determined," he said looking askance from her chart, his black stethoscope dangling from his white coat like a sleeping snake.

She strained to talk above a whisper, her gravelly voice saying, "I've had enough. I'm not afraid of death. I believe there is something more, something better…more permanent. Buddha, Jesus, the Great Spirit… perhaps they're all reflections of it, or maybe what's after is completely different… something totally unimaginable and beyond our comprehension. Either way, I'm ready." She then took several wet breaths and looked directly at the physician.

"Well let's not make any hasty decisions. Don't be so quick to give up," he said admonishing her.

"Doctor, I've had a remarkable life. For that I'm very thankful. I've danced, laughed, cried, loved and even hated. Now a part of me experiences the world through the eyes of my great grandchildren. I run swiftly on their legs, my heart beats strong with their passion for life. I am not, however, above being envious, wishing I could still laugh and find joy in the littlest things… and have the world be my unexplored playground filled with high-flying swings and long, fast, silver slides… sprinklers and sandboxes. I realized I was old when I lost that feeling." Looking exhausted she took several deep breaths and continued, "Lately I've taken time to imagine the world without me… and you know doctor, it looks fine… just fine. Besides, the world has become such a lonely pace. A computer connects you to someone a thousand miles away while your neighbor sits home alone all day and doesn't even know your name."

"We all would like to be young again. Unfortunately there is no easy way out of this world."

"You know when I was a girl it was different or at least it seemed to be, but… memories are such untrustworthy things. I know I sound like a cackling old hen, but the parties and fun we had when I was small... seemed so natural, part of our lives' very fabric. Every weekend neighbors came over to play music, sing and cook elaborate meals. The women traded recipes and stories of their children. The men would smoke cigars and play cards or bocce ball. They would talk about work and money and the war. We ran through the house making up a hundred different games. Nobody went without. If anyone had a need, someone was there… to visit or talk or bring food… baby-sit. You name it. We were our own social security," she said casting her eyes out the window, her feelings stirred momentarily by the resurrected memories. She inhaled deeply filling her lungs with oxygen, her soliloquy draining the small amount of energy she had left.

"Yes, Mrs. Antoni, the world is certainly a different place, but it's not all bad. Look at the wonderful things technology has done... new medicines... in fact, there is a new drug called Aventis that has been..."

"No... no... no more drugs. I don't want to wake up finding the soft textures against my face are clumps of my hair... or spend another beautiful summer day sick in the bathroom... no, I don't want to force a few more months out of this broken body. If anything I desire to hasten things."

"Are you implying..." Connors started as he removed his gold wire rimmed glasses and sat on the edge of the bed.

"Suicide doctor. A last self -directed act before becoming only an incoherent puppet covered with flesh and blood. Incapable of caring for myself... dependent completely on strangers. I don't want to be lying in bed... unable to... wishing I had..." There was a long silence in the room broken only by the sound of a pigeon fluttering its wings against the outside windowsill and bobbing its head while doing a frenetic dance, impassively looking at the city streets below, oblivious to the conversation inside the room.

"That's unethical... to assist you in such a way," Connors said looking sympathetically. Her eyes reddened and a tear slid gracefully along her cheek, her arm too feeble to wipe it away. Connors took a tissue and gently dabbed her face. He then looked into her eyes for a long time and saw the sadness and fear, the hopes and regrets that she collected over a lifetime.

"Sometimes the kindest thing to do is to help someone die," she said turning her eyes towards a worn photograph of her wedding day that she had removed from her purse. Then, the future was all in front of her but time had raced away from her so quickly, she had barely noticed, and now it was almost gone.

"Charlotte, you know I... there is no consent to murder. Palliative care has advanced to the point..."

She interrupted, "To the point where you need to suffer quite a bit before getting it. There are too many patients to be cared for... call lights go hours without being answered. People sit in their own excrement waiting for someone to come."

"I can assure you your needs would be met."

"Doctor, you cannot."

"You don't know me, Charlotte, but I can't be the judge of people's lives and what value they hold. I will leave you two tablets of a strong narcotic for pain... it will take a few hours for the nurses to get some stocked on the floor, and I don't want you to have to wait." He reached into his coat and opened a large vial, carefully removing two tablets and placing them on the cherry veneer nightstand. The cheap mauve table light flickered then went off.

She clumsily tried to reach up and touch his arm but the effort was too much. They talked a few minutes more. Before leaving, he reached down and gave her a long hug. She used her last bit of strength to reach around and hold him close to her. She smiled, thankful for the game she used to play with her grandfather. Shortly after she was again laughing and dancing at her birthday party. Her mother and father looked on with pride. Her new ring looked dazzling in the spring sunlight. Her grandparents fussed over her. She smiled as her old friends arrived, each taking a turn to greet her and hold her tightly. This time the day would never end.

THE WAGER

The doctor's office was crowded and hot. I could tell I had a long wait. There were a dozen places I'd rather be. Unfortunately I felt lousy and needed a checkup. The Band-Aid on my arm itched and reminded me of my recent blood draw. I sat away from the hacking and wheezing congregation, leaned back and tried to relax. At my age there was a lot I could think about. However, I thought about what I often thought about... especially in doctor's waiting rooms or funeral parlors; that event fifty years ago that changed the lives of six people, all in a very bad way.

We were young, on a fishing weekend along the Genesee River. As I recall, it was Frank who first made the suggestion. We thought it was a joke, but it turned to be the farthest thing from that we could ever imagine. It was a very dark night and Frank stood near the campfire, which burned brightly as orange embers danced and died in the crisp sky above him. With his beard he looked like the devil addressing the damned.

"Everyone listen... please... I have a proposal to make," he said getting our attention. "It's really more of a wager. Something I've thought about on occasion but never mentioned before." I shook awake my identical twin brother Jim, who had dozed off after a few of his favorite Corsendock pale ales.

"What is it Bob?" Jim asked looking at me with glazed eyes. I silently pointed towards the fire. Donald and Ed sat up and looked amusingly at Frank. A moment later, Mark appeared from a path in the woods with an armful of kindling wood. Perspiration caused his round face to glisten and he dropped his collection of dried twigs a few feet from the fire. He settled down with the rest of us and listened as Frank spoke.

"Please, allow me to speak plainly. We have been friends for many years. Let's face it gentlemen, our lives are merely a notch above the mundane. We have no formal education. We are common laborers and small business owners. Soon we'll have families to support. Our carefree days together will soon be past us. So, before that time, I propose a wager... to add a little excitement to our lives and a way for us to remain connected as the years pass and our lives take different paths."

"All right, get to it Frank! What's this big idea you have?" I shouted.

"Well Rob, here it is. First we all ante up one thousand dollars. I know that is a lot of money but hear me out. Every year we'll get together for a formal night out and each put in an additional thousand dollars. The last one alive collects it all. Every last cent. With a well-managed investment strategy we could be talking over a million dollars. It's more retirement money than social security is ever going to pay us. It also gives us an excuse to get together every year, at least once, to relive old times. It's also a hell of a good reason to quit smoking and start leading healthier lifestyles. We all need to do a bit of that." Murmurs rose up from the group; most of us were skeptical. In the end, however, after much talk and much beer, we all agreed to take the gamble. Greed had taken hold of us. Everyone believed they would be the last one standing.

Retirement seemed a million years away and dying seemed incomprehensible. A month later we enjoyed bottles of Chardonnay and oven poached red snapper with cream sauce. A man named John Devlin explained the financial details and formalities. He passed out graphs that explained all the investment options. It was all very professional. We each signed the papers and paid our first installment.

Gatherings continued like that for more than thirty years. Although our lives took divergent paths, the meetings gave us a chance to share our successes and our heartaches. The wager worked surprisingly well. It really accomplished what we all hoped it would. One day tragedy finally struck. Don and Mark were on their way to a hunting lodge. It was a bad winter's day. Don lost control of the car on a steep interstate hill. I was working in my body shop when I got the news. Death had never hit so close. Among muffled cries, we buried them on a bleak, frigid February morning. It was strange to not see them at the yearly meetings anymore, but eventually we grew accustomed to their absence. Some years after our get together finished, we would make a pilgrimage to Glenwood cemetery to pay our respects. The years passed and we continued our yearly social event. We watched the money grow to numbers that seemed hard to fathom.

Twelve years after the loss of Don and Mark, Frank lost his life in a freak accident. A car-jack slipped while he was changing his motor oil. He was found the next morning when his wife returned from a trip to visit her sister. That left Ed, my brother Jim, and me.

The Bull Market of the eighties pushed the value of our wager over a million dollars. Luckily we moved most of it into bonds before the NASDAQ plummeted. We continued to get together every year. Then came the untimely death of Ed after a routine appendectomy, some sort of heart arrhythmia did him in. So it was me and my twin Jim. We were both in great health. There was no medical reason we shouldn't make it well into our eighties before the Reaper paid his visit.

We joked since we were identical twins we would both die on the same day, leaving all the cash for our wives and their new boyfriends to blow. That might have been true had I not gotten him very drunk last night and smothered him with a pillow. His wife was in the hospital for knee surgery, and his son wouldn't find him before morning.

Retiring a millionaire while earning thirty thousand dollars a year with four children to raise requires shrewd thinking and some luck. I possessed both. When I rigged the brakes on Don's car the accident caused such a fire that nobody suspected a thing. The fire was a bit of luck. Taking the opportunity to kick out the car-jack on Frank was a brilliant move on my part … and the insulin in Ed's IV line helped move me closer to the payoff. That left only my brother, and a seventy-year-old man dying in his sleep is not totally unexpected.

The minutes dragged on in my family doctor's waiting room. As soon as I finish up with him I'll go home and wait for the call about Jim's unexpected demise.

"Mr. Lockley, please come to the front desk," the receptionist called out.

"Hello, I'm Robert Lockley," I responded seeing my exit finally in sight.

"Please go down to Dr. Hanston's office."

I entered taking a seat on a formal looking green leather sofa.

"Hello Bob," the doctor said peering up from my chart.

"Hello Doc, got an answer for me? Why have I been so damn tired?"

"I'm afraid I do. I'm not sure how to say this, but you have acute leukemia. Your blood work came back half an hour ago. A hematopathologist has confirmed it."

"Oh my God... how... what does that..." I stammered. I was completely in shock. My hands shook and I felt lightheaded.

"Normally that's pretty terrible news Bob, especially for someone your age ... survival is usually less than six months even with pretty harsh chemotherapy and radiation, but you have an ace in the hole my very fortunate friend. A bone marrow transplant from your twin brother Jim should give you better than ninety percent chance at a complete cure... not many people with that kind of luck," he said, smiling widely and looking much happier than I must have at that moment.

THE
UNDERTAKING

Some things are never forgotten, no matter how much time has passed. The chisel of life's experiences occasionally finds walls that are unbreakable. One such event I recall began on an early fall afternoon a few weeks after our high school education began. It was a crisp and sunny Saturday. The trees were not fully polychromatic, still harboring some of summer's green hue. It was a day filled with the unmistakable fresh scent of early autumn that is only truly appreciated by the young. The exuberance for life, usually lost by adulthood, leaves behind only an imperfect memory of those long past days of childhood. The smell of a new car or the thrill of buying a new house cannot match the giddiness of a brand new pair of sneakers, a day at the amusement park, or the first day of summer vacation. Any ten-year-old can attest to that fact.

It was our weekly pick up football game traditionally played on a long grass field that was adjacent to the neighborhood elementary school. St. Ignatius was the grade school where most of us spent our early years. Sam had just barreled into Jim preventing a touchdown and nearly forsaking him any progeny. While Jim moaned on the turf and grabbed his midsection, Donald, now the self-proclaimed referee stated authoritatively that the game was over. It was five o'clock and time to get home for dinner lest we risk suspension of our newly gained freedoms that came along with being a "high schooler".

On the way home we tossed the ball around pretending to be one or another of our local sports heroes. We talked about our new teachers, discussed how stern the principal was rumored to be and told stories of how upper classmen tried to embarrass one of the new kids at lunch. That's when Sam brought up the subject. The subject I secretly hoped would be forgotten.

"Well, we're in high school now, are we gonna do it?" he said tossing the ball to himself. "We always said we would."

"Do what?" I asked feigning ignorance, but knowing exactly what Sam was referring to.

"You know, like we always said we'd do once we got to high school," he answered impatiently.

"That was just talk," said Donald hoping to brush away the subject and get home to dinner. His father's drinking was enough to deal with. He didn't need this, It was a subject he was not comfortable with.

"It wasn't just talk," Jim interjected, then adding, "We said that when we started high school, we'd do it."

"Well, we didn't say exactly when, just that we would. High school is four years long, maybe longer for some of us," I said taking Donald's side of the argument. Donald was a bit slower than the rest and I often found myself defending him, though this time I had more selfish motives.

"You guys are chicken shit," Sam said.

"Hell we are," said Don with more defiance in his voice than usual. "Okay then," Donald continued, "If we do it then you're going in first, or are *you* chicken shit?"

"I'm not scared," retorted Sam.

"All right, we'll see smart-ass," said Donald, "We'll see." No one said another word. We got to the corner of Fourth Street and Sterling and each went our separate ways home. We would talk about doing *it* again I was sure. This was one topic that would not

191

die. I'm not even sure how it became a topic but it seemed to have made its way surreptitiously into our lives.

Jim McAlly's Uncle Jonathan owned a funeral home up on Palace Avenue. He was close to retirement and most of the day-to-day business was being handled by a large Jamaican fellow known simply as Mr. Toppi. The funeral home had an expansive blacktop parking lot. When not in use by mourners, it became the site of our Whiffle ball league or games of "strike out." In the winter the plowed mounds of snow became endless caverns for junior explorers. One summer we turned the garage into a makeshift gym when we decided weight training was necessary if we wanted pre-teen buffed bodies. My arms still ache thinking of the endless curls with 20 lb weights. It's clear to me now that the funeral home and the immediate environs were our local social club. But unlike your typical club, some areas were strictly off limits even to the highest-ranking member. The inside of the funeral home was such an area.

There was a dark green door with chipped paint that marked the entrance to a small annex attached to the main building. The window was heavily frosted preventing any view of what was rumored to be the embalming room, a room in which we imagined unspeakable things occurred. Anyone feeling brave could slowly climb the three stairs and try to peek inside. Pressing one's face close to the door when the sun was just right, a distorted glimpse of the forbidden room was possible. Inevitably we would hear a sound or imagine some movement inside that would send us scurrying back across the parking lot to the amusement of the less courageous cast of onlookers. One of the most fearless of our group was Tommy. He would sometimes strain at the window for several minutes before taking flight. Tommy was a few years younger than the rest of us, but always tried to act a bit older. He was a good kid and didn't have many friends his own age. His neighbors were mostly older folks who had retired from the steel mill.

Tommy lived outside of the immediate neighborhood and was therefore a more peripheral member of our group, which was affectionately known by our family members as "The Crew." Most of us lived in the north side of the city on side streets that sprouted from a long busy avenue. Main Street was home to movie theatres, barbershops, as well as a large variety of specialty clothing stores, department stores, and antique shops. There were also a variety of small, family owned restaurants, representing innumerable ethnic groups. Places like Bertha's and Louie's Texas Red Hots. There was Kostas for Greek food and Lombardo's restaurant for high end Italian cuisine. The side streets sported repetitive two family dwellings each having the same square plot of grass in both the front and back. Houses differed only in color and state of repair or in some cases disrepair. A short concrete driveway separated each residence and led to the inevitable two car detached garage in the backyard. No cars were ever actually parked in the garages mind you, even during bitter cold winters or particularly fierce snowstorms. They merely served as elaborate storage sheds for broken bicycles, discarded toys, rusted portable gas grills, and large rolled up rugs that were never used but religiously passed down from generation to generation in case someone might one day need them. The most creative used the garage as a recreational area complete with stove, portable T.V. and refrigerator with a picnic table for late night card games or a relaxing cup of coffee. There was only one unbreakable rule; no cars were allowed. That's what the driveway and street were for.

Tommy's mom would drop him off at one of our houses to spend the day. His family didn't have much money but that didn't stop him from being generous. His dad was away a lot and served in the army. He was even wounded once and had a purple heart for his troubles. Tommy often treated us to candy from Foley's Tobacco Shop. It was owned and run by Nicholas Foley, known to neighborhood kids as Mr. Nick. He was an old and kind gentleman who was the purveyor of such delicacies as Swedish Fish, Jawbreakers, an assortment of penny candies, and trading cards. His iron racks held various magazines, tabloids, and half a dozen newspapers. It was the place our parents sent us for a quart of milk or a pack of cigarettes… when selling them to twelve year olds was completely acceptable… on Saturday mornings. To our delight, he carried a large selection of exotic squirt guns. When these water cannons began appearing on Mr. Nick's shelves, it was as sure a sign as anything nature could muster, that summer had finally arrived. Mr. Nick's weathered but kind face was the one constant in the chaotic life of a city kid. There were always new teachers, new little league coaches, and all the changes inherent in growing up and older. Mr. Nick's smile, soft voice, and slow shuffle were a comfort we sought as much as the sweet delights in his shop. He always had a kind word and never failed to inquire about the well being of our parents and siblings. Neighbors said he owned that shop when our own parents were kids.

Monday afternoon we stopped by Mr. Nick's after school. After picking up some Freeze Pops we walked down Main Street towards Donald's house. He had some new turtles his mom had bought him and we wanted to have a look. On the way there Tommy told us he had come up with a plan, a plan for finally doing *it*.

"All right," he said "We each tell our parents we're spending Friday night at a friend's house. This way, we can hang out until dark and then we'll sneak in the funeral home. There's a window in the basement we can get in… and nobody leaves till we see a dead body." Tommy spoke with bravado that I didn't think any of the rest of us possessed. Friday was still four days away and I was already feeling ill. I freaked out last year when I had to go to my grandmother's wake. The sweet smell of the flowers and having to kneel at the coffin staring at her lifeless body, secretly praying I didn't see her take a breath or see her eyes open… all of it made my head swirl. The thought of sneaking into a funeral and seeing who knows what… I couldn't imagine it without giving myself a stomachache.

The week passed quickly and I thought of a dozen excuses why I couldn't participate. In the end, however, I found myself asking permission to spend the night at Donald's. If I didn't do this I would be the object of ridicule until I went to college. Don had permission to be at Jim's, Sam at my house and so on. That evening we grabbed hot dogs at Louie's Texas Red Hots then walked over to Mr. Nick's for an ice cream. We were disappointed to see a closed sign on the tobacco store for the second day in a row. We then decided to go straight to Jim's house where we played a few games of Stratego without much enthusiasm. Our thoughts were elsewhere, on other more sinister places. Eventually we took the long walk to Tommy's house to pick up the last participant in the night's nefarious activities.

Tommy came out of his house wearing only a windbreaker and looking a bit upset. He said his mom was in "a mood" and he suggested maybe she was "on her period." He overheard her talking to his grandmother about his dad coming home. A couple of times his dad's leave had been canceled at the last moment and this always got his mom in a tizzy. Tommy hoped this wasn't the case. He really missed his father and looked forward to seeing him again. He loved going to a movie with him and then getting ice cream. He wouldn't admit it but he loved when his dad tucked him in at night. It made him feel safe and helped melt away any worries or insecurities he harbored. He was proud when his father wore his uniform and the way people who didn't even know him sometimes shook his hand on the street and thanked him for his service. Vietnam wasn't a popular war, Tommy knew that, but people never let on if they felt that way when his father was in town. After some cajoling Tommy's mom eventually said it was okay for him to spend the night at a friend's house. He could go but she asked him to be home early. Tommy could still hear her whimpering when he left, secretly glad he wouldn't have to put up her antics this evening. He felt she was emotionally fragile and secretly wished she could be confident and strong like his father.

It was almost nine o'clock. The five of us walked up Main Street towards Palace Avenue. Tommy cupped his hands and whistled a few tunes as Sam and I kidded Donald about something or other. Jim dawdled behind kicking a flattened soda can down the street. At the corner of the next street we saw the green and white sign that said *The Jonathan Curak Memorial Funeral Home*. The reality of what we were planning to do was now in front of me, full force and without a chance to retreat. None of us would admit the fear we felt. Deep down I think we would have all liked to flee to the safety of our own homes and the protection of our parents. However nobody uttered a sound.

Jim led us up the driveway and around the back. I remember how differently and foreboding even familiar things looked in the blackness of night. Tommy grabbed my arm and pulled me to the front of the group. He pointed and said,

"The second window, the one with the crack in it. I loosened the frame up last week. It's not locked. We can get in that way."

"Donald's the skinniest so he should go first," I offered.

"No, send in Sam, if he can fit, we'll all be able to," Donald retorted. Sam was secretly regretting all of those double bacon cheeseburgers and thick vanilla shakes he loved so much. Down deep I'm sure he was less concerned about getting in quickly, and more concerned about getting out.

"All right, but I'm not going anywhere in there until the rest of you get inside," Sam said, his face looking pale and unsure.

"Deal," said Tommy who then pried out the window revealing a basement that resembled a black bottomless pit. Sam tried slipping in legs first and for a moment was stuck until Donald and Jim pushed his portly belly past the concrete window casement. All the while Donald mumbled and grunted with the occasional "Lard Ass", and "Sow" being the only intelligible words I could hear. Sam eventually slid to the bottom with an audible thud. I had hoped Sam would not make it through and we could end this evening and go to the bowling alley or play a game of space invaders. No such luck. Now it was time for the rest of us to join him. With some effort, each of us eventually shimmied our way down. The street had looked vacant and I was confident nobody had seen us break in. The police or dead bodies, I wasn't absolutely sure which would be worse to encounter.

The basement had an acrid smell that was new to me. I didn't realize it at the time, but it was the smell of death. After all, what does a thirteen-year-old really know about death? In all our games the dead got up and walked away at the end of the day. This was real death, permanent and unyielding. This was the place where the tears of aching grief were shed, where the inhabitants never ever again felt the warm touch or gentle embrace of a loved one and where good-byes were forever.

Donald turned on his flashlight allowing us to look around. The light bounced off cardboard boxes and stacks of old yellowed newspapers. Against the far wall were large canisters of pink fluid and jars containing creams we had never seen before. They were the cosmetics for the dead. Pasty flesh made to look vibrant again. There were boxes of large curved needles and thick rolls of plastic twine. I could only imagine what gruesome task they were used for. Just visible around the corner was a long corridor with several rooms. Like cattle, we were all drawn in that direction. Nobody spoke above a nervous whisper. The flashlight revealed each room was sealed by a closed door. We carefully looked in the first room. Donald, with a trembling hand slowly turned the knob. The door was unlocked and opened easily. The inside was frigid. We crowded out each other to look inside. Two metallic tables stood at the far end of the room. Large glass containers with worn yellow hoses were attached along each table's side. At the end of each hose was a large bore needle. At this point I'd seen enough and was ready to leave.

"I don't see any stiffs in here," Sam said. "Let's check the other rooms. Nobody leaves until we see a body. The plastic stuff has to be off, too. We need to see a face. Just a hand doesn't count." No one said a word as we moved quietly down the hallway and peered into the second room.

"Look over there," Donald called out. Our heads snapped up to see a body lying on a long metal table silhouetted by the flashlight's beam at the far end of the room. We looked at each other and Sam said,

"Come on, let's go! Nobody leaves now. We're not coming back another night so let's do it." He took the flashlight from Donald and slowly led the group into the room. I saw the light flickering and noticed Sam's hand was trembling. He stopped. His breathing was deep and audible. "I can't do this, Let's get out of here!" Sam gasped as he turned to leave.

"Wait, I'll do it." Tommy's voice came from the back of the group. "We planned this for years, we can't leave now." Although none of us would admit it, we envied Tommy's bravery. He certainly was gaining credibility in the group. Tommy took the flashlight from Sam and moved towards the table. The rest of us stood at the doorway or just outside the room. There was complete silence except for the thudding of our hearts. We watched incredulously as Tommy approached the motionless body.

Tommy stood next to the shrouded corpse. A smudge of red was visible just beneath the plastic covering. He reached down and pulled out his pocket knife. He carefully began to cut away the thick plastic. We all held our breath. Sam and Jim turned away. Tommy slowly pulled the shroud from around the face tearing parts of it away with his hands. By this time all of us had backed out of the room leaving Tommy alone with the corpse. I could see a wet stain on Donald's crotch but was too frightened to laugh at him. Sam and Jim were at the window trying to climb out. A moment later we heard a piercing scream… then Tommy yelling, "No… no… no." Everyone was startled. My first instinct was to run but I couldn't leave Tommy alone in that room. Everyone else was down the hall and Jim was still frantically trying to climb out the window. I turned back fighting the powerful urge to flee as fast as possible. It was then I entered the room and saw Tommy on one knee sobbing inconsolably, holding the hand of his fallen father.

I am afraid I have a confession to make. I misled you. I know that is a terrible thing for an author to do to a reader but it's been done and there is no going back. There is no use crying over spilled blood, is there? In my defense I must say that those of you who have read the stories in this sordid collection must have realized that nothing is as it seems. What appears real often turns out to be a fantasy and real motives often don't reveal themselves before it is too late. The truth is a murky thing often found alone shivering in a dark corner or whimpering under a blood stained shroud. It is often cloaked in a lie or can be found eviscerated on an autopsy table or perhaps buried in a makeshift grave in a stretch of lonely woods. Sometimes it beats imperceptibly in the moldering heart of a reanimated decaying corpse or is hidden in the flesh of man's best friend. That is also true of this book itself. It also has an unexpected ending. There are not thirteen stories after all. I just happen to like that number. You have to admit that the number thirteen carries a certain panache with it. There is, it turns out, a fourteenth story. I hope this is not an unwelcome turn of events. It is the narrative of two brothers one of whom happens to be a rather nasty serial killer laced with more than a pinch of psychopathy. Since I have deceived you I hope that you'll accept this story as a token of my sincere remorse. It is a saga of redemption and of brotherly love conquering what seemed like an insurmountable obstacle, or is it? I guess you'll have to read *Visit to the Asylum* to find out. I hope you find it a pleasant tale. Can I however make one small suggestion? Leave the light on as you read because you never know in what hidden corner or dark closet the truth might be lurking. Enjoy and best wishes for a restful night's repose.

VISIT TO THE ASYLUM

When my mother passed away last year it left just me… and my brother Jason. He however was not someone that we talked about. His affliction and that is exactly what the psychiatrists called it, had brought shame and heartbreak to our family. It led to us being ostracized from the community our ancestors lived and worked in for six generations. Perhaps if we lived in a large city it would have been politely overlooked or been buried among the hundreds of other outrages the populace was exposed to in any given year. We did not live in a big city. Therefore we bore the brunt of the community's disdain, although none of us could have done anything to prevent it. I considered leaving town but felt an obligation to help care for my distraught parents. Over the course of several years I finished a degree online and eventually secured a job that allowed me to work from home and became quite wealthy. Being a bachelor and having no children my expenses were minimal. This afforded me the luxury of isolating myself from judging eyes and malevolent comments of those in town who somehow blamed my family for the terrible events that occurred. Mother always believed the stress led to my father's passing at the age of fifty-five. He looked seventy in the casket. I don't expect the story I will tell on these pages will have many believers. I cannot let that stop me. By my solemn oath the words I write are the truth or so closely allied with it that it is one and the same in all the important particulars. The year was 1993 and it was a warm spring in Perrysburg, N. Y. I had just turned twenty-one. That's when the first body was discovered. It was down by Mill's creek about four miles from town center. Under brush and covered with shale she was found. It was Kaitlyn Strauss the fifteen year old daughter of the town's pastor. She was dressed in a bright blue Pinafore dress with some of the small white flowers caked in a mixture of blood and mud. Her face was bloated and was a peculiar shade of gray. Her left eye was nothing more than thick yellow jelly plastered to her cheek, at least that's what the rumors said.

The townsfolk were already agitated and when the results of the autopsy came back from the Monroe county medical examiner, things progressively got worse. There were signs of torture and the cause of death was manual strangulation. As could be predicted more patrol cars were on the street, children were subjected to strict curfews and doors were compulsively locked. Parties were cancelled and people looked across their shoulders whenever they heard footsteps in the night. Unfortunately this was not enough. Seven weeks later the body of Janine Casper, a fourteen year old foster child was discovered behind the barn of the Krienholdt dairy farm. The police said the body was bruised and beaten so badly that the parents could not identify her at the county morgue. It wasn't until dental records were matched that they knew for sure. The next year brought two more homicides. The FBI was recruited to help find what the local paper dubbed "the madman of the meadows." We all watched the crime scenes on the news. Investigators clad in white paper suits collecting trace evidence, photographing bodies and giving occasional press releases. It was eighteen months later after the seventh murder that my brother was arrested. The community was shocked. He was a top student and varsity letterman in soccer. There was never a hint of trouble in his past. His IQ was above 150 and most people thought he would be one of the great success stories from our rural community. Friends, teachers, clergymen and former coaches all professed their shock and dismay on the six o'clock news. Our family became hermits and for weeks afterward my father rarely left his room.

The trial lasted four weeks and there was ironclad DNA evidence that tied Jason to the murders. Several psychiatrists from New York City testified he suffered from schizophreniform disorder and would have intermittent bouts of delirium and psychosis. Although most people didn't buy it enough jurors were convinced that he was found innocent due to insanity and was remanded to the Addison county psychiatric unit's forensic ward. This was located ninety miles away but might as well have been on another continent. "He got away with murder," was the phrase we heard most often. My father refused his son's name ever be spoken in his presence. Editorials slammed the verdict and tore holes in the jurors' reasoning. The law however is the law and one early fall morning he was loaded into a police van and driven to Addison's. That was thirteen years ago. There was never any communication between us until I unexpectedly received a letter from him.

At first my hands trembled as I held it tightly and stared at the return address label. Pacing the first floor of my apartment, I truly considered burning it or tearing it to shreds. I placed it on my desk and for days passed it without touching it. It sat like an unwanted visitor lurking in the shadows. It cajoled me and haunted my dreams until finally… I opened it. I was surprised at the gentleness of the words. I guess I shouldn't have been too shocked. I am sure all mail sent by the patients was screened. The letter contained no ranting or hatred for abandoning him. There were no acrimonious tirades. There was only understanding and acceptance.

He talked about the insight that the psychotherapy sessions he regularly attended afforded him. He extolled the great benefits his medications such as risperidone and ziprasidone provided. He understood the nature of his crimes made it unlikely he would ever be released back into society. He did however want to reconnect on some level with me. To form some bond no matter how weak between us. After he was informed of our mother's death he understood there was now only the two of us. He realized how strained the relationship might be at first but hoped over time we could build something between us.

He repeated several times that he was no longer the mentally disturbed person who carried out the heinous crimes which had destroyed our family and many others. He asked if I would consent to pay him a visit. He would understand if I refused. It was something I had not done in over thirteen years. As you might guess I struggled with this concept. I debated back and forth for almost a fortnight. I had spent well over a decade burying the idea that I even had a brother and denying to myself and anyone else that I had even the most remote concern for his wellbeing. Now I was confronted with a choice. In the end I decided I would pay him a visit if only to satisfy my own curiosity about him. I needed to find out if his transformation was real or only a fantasy that I secretly wished were true.

After completing my day's work I had a light supper and set out for the psychiatric facility that was often referred to in derogatory terms as the asylum, the madhouse, or the state lunatic hospital by the locals. It was just past seven p.m. when I pulled my car into the visitor's parking lot. I passed by several majestic maple trees and a few oak trees that lined the walkway leading to the institution. About thirty yards away was a large pond in which bobbed and floated a single rowboat loosely harnessed to the muddy shore by a cast iron stake. A steel gated kennel containing several intimidating Caucasian Mountain Shepherds was anchored to a limestone storage building. The main building was connected to two expansive adjacent wings. They were joined together by high red brick octagonal towers. At the top of one was a belfry, which rang with a somber toll on the hour. About a hundred yards to the left of the main complex was a cemetery enclosed by a tall black gate. At several spots the rusted fence had collapsed in on itself. It housed stones that appeared to traverse more than a century of death. According to the map I brought most of the institute's other buildings were connected by a haphazard and confusing labyrinth of underground tunnels and cobblestone passageways. I approached the oversized front windows of the central building. Adjacent to the palladium window was a flowering dogwood that looked near death and had been ravaged by some parasite or other. The arched Victorian pine door led me into the two story foyer. I registered as a visitor and received a red plastic pass to attach to my shirt. I was asked to take a seat as Dr. Franz Clauberg wanted to speak with me before I met my brother. I was now growing somewhat anxious and wondered if I had made the right choice in coming. I seriously considered just walking out and burning all future correspondence I might receive. I took several deep breaths and tried to relax myself. After feeling slightly more grounded I leafed through a few outdated magazines and eventually just sat back on the tufted brown leather chair to wait. My mind wandered and then I remembered where I had heard that name before… Clauberg. I read about him about six months back. He had been investigated for some kind of Medicare fraud but was eventually acquitted. Some newspaper accounts said it was because he was smart enough to cover his tracks while others argued he was an innocent victim of an overzealous bureaucracy. There was even some suggestion his father had served in the Dachau concentration camp but that was never proven. It was alleged he had incurred some very sizeable debts, an acrimonious divorce and gambling problems being the contributing factors, if I remembered correctly. I began to wonder about the quality of mental healthcare my brother was receiving. I then saw a tall thin elderly man wearing a stylish blazer with a bright yellow shirt and blue tie walking my way. "Hello, Mr. Foster?" he asked with a wide smile and heavy German accent.

"Yes, I'm Mathew Foster, Jason's brother," I said as I reached out to shake his hand. I nervously rubbed my beard as I appraised the distinguished physician standing before me. He seemed reserved but friendly.

"I am Dr. Clauberg. I've been the main psychiatrist working with your brother since his arrival almost a decade and a half ago. Although we have a team approach here I am primarily responsible for organizing his therapy sessions, charting his progress and adjusting his medications. I make all the treatment recommendations."

"I'm glad to meet you. I'm sure there is a lot to talk about."

"There certainly is but all in good time. I must commend you on your bravery in coming here. I know the circumstances are not ideal but I truly believe that reconnecting with your brother will go a very long way in aiding his recovery. I know he is excited to see you again and very happy to have you visit. We've spoken of it all week." Dr. Clauberg then took a seat next to mine and gave me a brief summary of what transpired over the years. He described the long road Jason has travelled to get to his present state. He seemed to be doing very well on his current medication regimen and was more engaged than ever in the social and vocational training that was offered. His reaching out to me seemed to be the next major step in his recovery; that at least is what the good doctor thought. We proceeded through a maze of corridors and passed three locked doors into the forensic unit which housed the most violent and mentally unstable patients. Several seemed to be walking about in a fog while others were tied to chairs with a Posey restraint. Dr. Clauberg always referred to them as patients and never inmates even though most of them would never see the outside world again except through a barred window. The occasional banging and screams coming from some of the rooms was unsettling although Dr. Clauberg seemed impervious to them. I silently wondered how my brother could have tolerated thirteen years in this abysmal prison for the mentally deranged. We finally arrived at room 2326, the one housing my brother. He rapped on the door several times then slid his nametag through a magnetic detector and a few seconds later there was a loud snap and the portal slowly opened. I gazed in through the partially opened door and saw my brother sitting quietly on his bed. The only other furniture in the room was a small table and chair and a steel toilette with overlying sink. A small barred window let in a modicum of the quickly fading sunlight. He stood up and slowly walked toward me. There was unquestionably tension filling the room but a moment later we hugged each other and we were both in tears. I sat in the chair and Jason on the bed. Dr. Clauberg stood inconspicuously at the far end of the room to make sure things went smoothly. We spoke for about thirty minutes. I told him about my success as an online businessman and how I was planning to move out of town into a new house. He spoke of his long road out of darkness to a place where he felt in control of himself. The future was not going to be perfect but it looked better to him. Eventually we said good-bye and I promised to visit again.

I did visit many times over the next year. Contrary to what I initially thought would happen we actually grew close. There were many times I forgot why my brother was housed here. When I remembered I sometimes grieved thinking what a wonderful business partnership we might have had. I silently wished our lives had taken a different path. My brother was very intelligent and eventually with Dr. Clauberg's blessing I taught Jason accounting and book-keeping as part of the vocational training program the patients were required to attend. Although it was against the rules to pay him he essentially became my partner of sorts. Over time he learned enough to balance the books and we often discussed different ideas to increase business opportunities and maximize profits. Giving him an outlet for his creativity was very helpful to him. Dr. Clauberg said Jason's bouts of depression were becoming infrequent and his ability to concentrate and participate in social activities at the hospital was increasing.

It was the middle of November when I next stopped to visit. Thanksgiving was fast approaching. I had pictures of the new house

I wanted to show him. Dr. Clauberg called to me as I pushed the elevator button. "Mathew!"

I turned to look as Clauberg grabbed my arm. "We have to talk before you visit today."

"Is there a problem?" I was concerned by the look on his face.

"Jason has been acting out this week. He had to be restrained several times. He screams about being innocent and set up and rants how he doesn't belong here. He was violent with several of the staff. He needed to be strongly medicated on several occasions. I believe his interactions with you have shone a light on all that he's missed. The life he could have shared with you. He now sees all the things he will never experience. I believe his emotional outbursts are part of the healing process and something he must work through. It isn't necessarily a bad thing because in the end he must come to understand there are limits to the kind of life he can lead."

"Do you think I shouldn't visit?" I was suddenly unsure of what to do. I felt a little panicked.

"No… not at all. I think this is something he must confront. It is a new reality for him. I just wanted you to be prepared. We had to move him to an isolation room until he is no longer a threat to any of the other patients or staff. I am the only person working with him until things settle down. Don't be afraid. He looks different and will seem more agitated, but underneath he's still your brother. As hard as it might be please try to remember that."

"All right. Then can I see him now?"

"Yes of course. I appreciate your understanding the situation. We have to take the south corridor. That's where the isolation wing is." We then travelled through several rundown tunnels and sidestepped a few mice. We finally got to an elevator which we took to the seventh floor. This part of the institute was particularly inhospitable. The furniture was in disrepair and many of the lights had burned out. Abandoned wheelchairs sat unattended in corners. I hoped my brother would not have to be here long. I couldn't imagine how this would contribute to his mental wellbeing. We finally reached his room and Clauberg had to open it with a key. There were no fancy electronic latches here. I was shocked by what I saw. My brother was restrained to a bed, his eyes bloodshot and looking as if he hadn't slept in a week.

"Go to him. Tell him you're here. It will calm him."

"Jason… Jason it's Matt. I know things are bad now but I promise I will help you get better. I promise not to leave you." There was no response. He stared blankly at the ceiling.

Dr. Clauberg looked at his watch and stepped closer to me. "Mathew, It's almost six o'clock. Let me get you a sandwich and some coffee. Talk to him gently. He hears you even if he doesn't respond. The times you feel you have the least to give is the times he needs you most. For safety, keep your distance. I'll be back in a moment." I tried to appear calm but wasn't sure what to say. There were long bouts of silence. I just talked about how much I enjoyed seeing him and looked forward to when he was feeling better so we could go back to running the business together. I checked my watch several times. I wanted to leave but didn't want to abandon my brother. After about ten minutes Dr. Clauberg finally returned.

I nervously wolfed down the ham sandwich and cup of coffee. I felt the stress was finally getting to me. My head spun. The room started going out of focus and I felt unsteady. Soon the room went black.

I awoke and everything was hazy. I fought against the straps, my knuckles white and sweat beading on my forehead. I felt the veins in my neck filled with blood. It was no use. I couldn't move. I gave up and collapsed back onto the bed. To my surprise my reflection in the sheen of the door showed I was now clean shaven. I heard voices but it was unclear who was talking. My arms felt heavy and tingled from the constricting straps. I squinted several times to clear my vision. That's when I saw my brother standing at the end of the room talking to Dr. Clauberg. He was wearing my clothes and what looked like a fake beard. After he finished a short conversation with Clauberg he turned toward me.

"Well hello, brother. How are you doing? You had a nasty fall off that chair. I'm glad you didn't hurt yourself seriously. Doc put you in those restraints for your own safety."

"What the hell's going on? Why are you wearing my clothes? Who in God's name shaved me?"

"Isn't that one of the perks of having a twin brother? So you can swap clothes… and as luck, well not really luck… actually a lot of really detailed planning… would have it, swapping lives. This switch of living arrangements is going to cost you a pretty penny Mathew. Doc here is going to get a nice chunk as well, but I think I deserve the rest. Don't worry I promise to visit. I might not even wait thirteen years to make the first one… but I'll have to think about that. I might be reluctant to leave that beautiful new house of mine."

"No… no! I'm innocent. I've been set up. Somebody help me!" In an instant Clauberg put a needle in my arm and everything faded away. When that happens it's usually hours before I wake up.

I've been here almost four years now. No visitors. Clauberg keeps a close eye on me and if I get unruly I know the needle will be there shortly. Because I'm considered violent I almost see nobody but him. No one believes what I tell them anyway. I secretly write these letters but they're always found and make it only as far as the nearest trash can. Perhaps someday someone will see me as more than a raving lunatic. Occasionally I find a discarded newspaper to read or catch a bit of the local news. It seems a few bodies have turned up in Genesee County. I guess it's true that no matter how much money you have, in the end everyone returns to the profession they know best.

About the Author

Michael Albert is a lifelong resident of western New York. He grew up in north Buffalo and was educated at St. Margaret's grammar school and is a graduate of St. Joseph's Collegiate Institute. He earned a B.S. in Biology from the University of Dallas and spent five months travelling Europe during his sophomore year as part of the University's academic program. He was awarded his Doctorate in Medicine from Albany Medical College in 1986 and subsequently completed a residency in pathology at the University of Rochester Medical Center. He is a diplomate of the American Board of Pathology and certified in both anatomic and clinical pathology. He is a founding member of Eastern Great Lakes Pathology and X-Cell Laboratory of Western New York. He also serves as the chairman of the pathology department at Buffalo Mercy Hospital. He received Mercy Hospital's physician of distinction award in 2010 and recently served as vice president and then president of the hospital's medical staff. He has had a lifelong interest in writing fiction, particularly in the genre of horror and suspense. His short story *The Knock on the Door* was selected as one of three winners of the 2013 Buffalo News short story competition. He credits his first attempts at writing to his high school English teacher, Gerald Newman, who required daily journal writing as part of the courses he taught. Dr. Albert is happily married to his wife Melissa. They have five wonderful and energetic children and an assortment of dogs who keep life from ever becoming mundane. He and his family reside in the town of Orchard Park, New York.